HARD COUNTRY

D1599393

HARD COUNTRY

Chad Merriman

This Large Print edition is published by BBC Audiobooks Ltd, Bath, England and by Thorndike Press®, Waterville, Maine, USA.

Published in 2004 in the U.K. by arrangement with Golden West Literary Agency.

Published in 2004 in the U.S. by arrangement with Golden West Literary Agency.

U.K. Hardcover ISBN 0–7540–9990–3 (Chivers Large Print)
U.K. Softcover   ISBN 0–7540–9936–9 (Camden Large Print)
U.S. Softcover   ISBN 0–7862–6311–3 (Nightingale)

The text of this Large Print edition is unabridged.
Other aspects of the book may vary from the original edition.

Set in 16 pt. New Times Roman.

Printed in Great Britain on acid-free paper.

British Library Cataloguing in Publication Data available

Library of Congress Control Number: 2003116422

CHAPTER ONE

Duff Doncaster said in a quick undertone, 'Take it easy!' Even while his voice died away, he knew it fell on deaf ears. Hob's eyes had gone wide with the shock of recognition. There had been a second of bright, deadly liveliness in them. Now they were flat and fixed on the gangling man Hob had blocked on the crowded street of this raw river town of Dalles City.

Recognition hadn't yet come to the man, no inkling that his life would never again be the same. He only moved to step around Hob and go on. This was a teeming, motley town of men on the move. Many were rowdy roughnecks who enjoyed the practice of discourtesy. The man seemed used to that and to deferring instead of letting himself be baited into a ruckus. He grinned uneasily and shunted again, only to be blocked once more.

'Howdy, Vince Mounts,' Hob said finally. 'Long time no see.'

Mounts' mouth dropped open. He said uncertainly, 'You got me at a disadvantage, mister. I know you?'

'Don't see how you could forget me,' Hob said. 'Even after ten years.'

That did something so forceful to Mounts he lifted a hand and shuffled back a step. He

1

said dismally, 'Ten—years.'

'Puts us back on the trail from the Missouri,' Hob said with a slight grin. 'Don't it, Mounts?'

'You—were in the wagon company.' Duff had seen sick men and men in despair. Now he saw both in the same person. Mounts' gaze cut to Hob's hip. No gun hung there presently. The worn place showed that one often did. 'You're that boy of Burley Loman's.'

'Well, I was,' Hob said. 'Till you all hung him.'

Mounts stood weakly silent while he ran bleak eyes along the street. This was changing its pace as the late fall day turned into early night. But Mounts hadn't changed much, Duff thought. Maybe there hadn't been much there to change. He had been the weakest of them, a hanger-on of the others. But that had made him no less vicious in the end. Maybe it had made him more so.

Mounts said in an all-gone voice, 'They took you to California. What you doing up here?'

'Brought in cattle,' Hob said. 'Me and my partner. You ought to remember Duff Doncaster. His folks took me under their wing after you and yours made a orphan of me.'

Mounts glanced at Duff. Recognition brought him no comfort. He could remember two half-grown boys, meeting on the trail but like brothers from there on. Like brothers still since they were together after so many years. Identification only split the specter Mounts

2

saw into a double image. He looked again along a street indifferent to his distress.

It was the main street, cluttered with the trappings of a town whose life blood was traffic, travelers by the tens of thousands and freight by the thousands of tons. Highwheelers stood along the far side, backed to the loading platforms of stores and warehouses. The sidewalks were jammed by men on a thousand quests, some of them soldiers on pass from Fort Dalles.

Still searching the distance as though for help, Mounts said, 'Cattle, is it? Delivering to somebody?'

'Own 'em,' Hob said. 'Aim to winter here, anyhow. Maybe settle if the country turns out as good as Pike Pelton described it when I run into him in 'Frisco last spring.'

'Pelton!' The word ripped out of Mounts. 'I might have known it!'

Duff stared in amazement at a frightened man surrendering to panic. Mounts sidled away as if afraid even to turn his back. Instead of losing himself in the crowd, he only moved down a few doors. Then he cut into a cubbyhole place whose overhead sign said: MANDY'S QUICK EATS. Duff's vision settled on the sign, Mounts momentarily forgotten. Could it be? It surely could. If Mounts was here in Dalles City, the others were also. Duff felt himself turning cold. Finding Vince Mounts here hadn't been the quirk of chance he had thought until that moment.

Hob voiced one of the questions crowding Duff's mind. 'Mandy?'

'You reckon that's the little yellowhead who stole your heart on the trail?'

'Don't try to throw dust in my eyes,' Duff snapped. 'It was you seen Pelton, not me. He must've told you them people were here, and you never said a word about that to me. How come? Scared I wouldn't come in with you on the deal if I knew?'

'Mounts sure thought Pelton told me, anyhow,' Hob said with satisfaction. 'And that it's why we're here.'

'Did he or didn't he?' Duff insisted. 'And is it or isn't it?'

Behind the amusement in Hob's eyes there was a queer, intense light. 'Well, he might have mentioned them. And maybe I neglected to tell you, we had so much else on our minds. But don't worry about it. We're here to go into the cattle business like we planned.'

'You better mean that, Hob,' Duff warned.

'I mean it. But I won't deny it was satisfying to scare him out of his wits. And his kith and kin when they hear about it. You don't begrudge me that, do you?'

'Not if it's enough to satisfy you.'

Hob slid off at a tangent, the way he always did when something made Duff lock horns. 'What you feel like doing tonight?' he asked.

4

'Man told me they got some real nice gals at the dance hall. How about giving 'em a few whirls?'

Duff frowned into the gathering night. They were to have gotten in touch with Pelton on reaching Dalles City. Now the cattle were on Cripple Creek, off in the highlands south of town. But when they rode to town that afternoon, it had been to learn that Pelton was off up the country, with no set time for his return.

Duff said, 'Try your luck. I reckon I'll ride back to camp.'

'Always fretting over the steers.'

'Everything we've got's tied up in 'em,' Duff retorted. 'I hope you don't forget that.'

Hob frowned. 'That little business seems to have boogered you as bad as it did Mounts.'

'I don't understand you not telling me.'

'They've got nothing to do with you.'

'They've got plenty to do with me,' Duff returned. 'You're my partner. And friend.'

'Sure I am. And that's how it'll stay.'

Hob grinned, clapped Duff's shoulder, and hurried off along the sidewalk. He was big as Burley had been, which was big enough to stand out in any crowd. Duff turned the other way, thinking that size wasn't the only way Hob resembled the wild man who came to such a violent end on the trail. He knew he was asking a lot more restraint from his friend than was required of himself.

5

Even so, he meant to demand it of Hob. He liked what he had seen and learned of this raw, rockbound town sprung up in the middle of nowhere. Its main function had been and still was the accommodation of men and goods bound for other parts. Desert lay east, mountains west, with only the Columbia River to give it a hold on life. That had been enough, the river and now the gold that had boomed the whole interior.

Fort Dalles and its reservation used up the flat under a nude mountain spurring from the Cascades. Before the fort there had been Indians, traders and church missions there. In season there had been countless emigrant camps, for this had been as far as wagons could make it on the Oregon Trail. Here the great emigrations, the sagebrush country behind, had taken to rafts for the long, dangerous journey down through the gorge to the Willamette of their dreams. The spot had history, sure enough, but forgot it in its haste to make more. For now a backwash of the emigrations was on, a reverse flow of humanity now coming *up* the river.

Duff found he had passed the large, three-story hostelry that called itself Umatilla House and perched on the edge of the river. Immediately downstream were the long portage tramway and the wharf-boats of the river port. The *Oneonta,* a sidewheeler of five hundred tons, rode blandly on the river. Below

6

her the smaller *Idaho* was tied up for the night. Neither had long been in from its daily run downriver to the steam portage at the Cascades. They had a steam portage here now, too, fifteen miles of narrow-gauge track on which ran scaled-down engines and cars, extending for fifteen miles above Dalles City. The two little railroads, the first in the vast Northwest, had bypassed rock barriers. Now the river was open to navigation as far inland as the central Idaho mines.

But there were many mining localities that couldn't be served directly by the river. To meet their needs, Ben Holladay's overland stages, operated locally by Hailey & Greathouse, left daily for Boise Basin and Salt Lake City. The Canyon City Stage Line had tri-weekly service to the mining camps of the John Day. Wagon trains swarmed over the same crude roads, and pack strings still struck out from Dalles City for even remoter regions.

Pike Pelton had got his start during the long campaign against the Indians that had opened the interior to white people. There had been numerous forts and camps served out of Dalles City, and he had wangled some fat army supply contracts. Now, with that over and the gold fever raging, he was one of the overland freighters to the mining camps. But in San Francisco, when he saw Hob, Pelton had talked cattle.

It was a trade already pioneered, Pelton had

7

said. But there was plenty of room, for it took good men to put it over. The coastal valleys, he said, swarmed with cattle sprung from farm stock brought overland with the wagon trains or up from California. Natural fertility, the mild climate, and the grass-rich valleys west of the mountains had multiplied this early stock far beyond what could be consumed locally. The excess had become a menace. It couldn't be gotten rid of short of shooting, and it kept multiplying.

And beyond the mountains and an often waterless desert where Indians still racked around in spite of the reservations provided for them, beyond the hazards of weather, the treacheries of man and the fickleness of fortune, was a new population as short on beef as it was long on gold dust. In the Cariboo, on the Little Blackfoot, the Salmon and Clearwater, in Boise Basin, on the John Day, the Powder, the Owyhee . . . These weren't mining camps but regions, each with its scores of rich camps.

The coastal farmers were as short on money as they were long on beef, but the hazards of trying to reach this hungry market discouraged them. So they were happy to sell to a man not so readily discouraged, and he could about name his own price. In consequence, a beef steer bought in the valley, driven over the mountains to winter on bunchgrass and delivered to the mines as early as possible in

8

the spring could return a tenfold profit on the investment.

'That's right,' Hob had insisted when Duff doubted it. 'Pike said a fifteen dollar steer on the coast is a hundred-fifty dollar steer in the Cariboo the next spring. If—' And Hob had been realistic enough to grin. 'If you can get him there on the hoof. And yourself there with him.'

It was the kind of venture to set Hob on fire. They had made a stake from a silver claim in Nevada and were in San Francisco looking for something else to try. So Duff had agreed, and the stake had gone into a thousand head of cattle. Now that he was in it, Duff was in all the way, for they barely had enough left to carry them through the winter. It was a poor time to learn that Hob might have had another ax to grind, at the same time . . .

Duff found that he had reached the western edge of town. There he admitted what had really kept him from getting his horse and heading for camp as soon as he parted from Hob. He knew it would be better to let that matter sleep, also. Yet he had wondered until it was a curiosity too great to ignore. Turning, he walked back along the street to the heart of town.

The minute he stepped into the tiny, short-order eating house, he wanted to haul around and step right out again. The place proved to be empty except for the yellow-haired girl beyond the pineboard counter. He had hoped to have a cup of coffee, with enough others present to let him have his look without being conspicuous. But retreat was out of the question. She had already looked up at him. So he went on in. She was giving him a queerly intent look when he lifted his tall frame onto a stool. His heart felt like a wild pigeon in his chest.

Vince Mounts had come in here. Yet he must not have told her about Hob Loman showing up in the town. Except for that faintly bothered expression, she gave no sign of recognition. She came over in front of him, smiled in a businesslike way, and said, 'Evening, mister. What'll it be for you?'

'A cup of—!'

She fairly exploded. 'Why—Duff Doncaster!'

He grinned weakly and said, 'Howdy, Mandy.'

'Duff—oh, Duff! It's you!'

She thrust her hands across the counter, and he took them in his hard brown paws. Hers were strong hands and calloused. She hadn't had it easy, herself. Tears filled her eyes, and they were the same wonderful eyes he had remembered ten long years. But the thin, twelve-year-old body was now a woman's full-bloomed. The tomboy face was pretty and fully feminine. And alive with happiness.

'I kept trying to find you,' she said, as though it were yesterday. 'Till we got to Fort

10

Hall and the California people split off.'

'I dodged you, Mandy,' Duff said.

'I know. I understood, sort of. We were friends, but nothing like you and Hob. And it was my father who bore witness.'

Not wanting to talk about that, Duff said, 'Hob's along. I thought Vince Mounts told you.'

'Vince was in here. But I was too busy to talk to him, so he left. What happened?'

'We run into him on the street. It unsettled him.'

'No wonder. He tied the rope.'

Awareness hit Mandy then, slower in coming than it had come to Mounts because she didn't have all those guilty fears. She looked at him with eyes from which the excitement died away. But before she could speak again, a man came in. He wanted a sandwich and coffee, and Mandy took her time filling the order. Duff knew from her steadily more somber face that she was using the interruption to get her bearings. They were confused enough, for they involved the rights and wrongs of justice as some men saw it.

The legality of the trial they gave Burley Loman had never been in dispute. In those days, before the army brought law to the emigrant trails, the rules of the sea had been held to prevail. Under them more than one train captain had convened a court, as Dan Ragan, her uncle, had. Under them more than one convicted man had swung from upended wagon tongues, as Burley Loman had. On the dry, hot, treeless slopes west of South Pass. With only one grown friend left in the company, or friend of sorts. Pike Pelton, who defended him and pleaded for banishment rather than hanging.

Dan Ragan, Frank Fleeson, Vince Mounts —judge, witness and hangman. That was what Mandy was thinking about.

She served the man his order, then came back to Duff. 'Should Vince have been scared?' she said quietly.

'I wish I could answer that,' Duff said truthfully. 'I never had the faintest notion you and your family were here. But Hob found out. He seen Pike Pelton in San Francisco.'

'Pelton?'

'Mounts took that for bad news, too. How come?'

Mandy said quickly, 'No reason.'

Duff heard the door open again. Her eyes switched toward it, and he saw her suck in a quick breath.

CHAPTER TWO

The man who came in from the street was grayer of hair than he had been back there on the trail. If the lincs of his face had been deepened by the years, they had only set the sternness of it and its hint of self-certainty. His eyes slid instantly to Duff and went harder. The instant recognition, relating the man he saw with the gangling boy of the trail, showed he had heard from Vince Mounts. He pushed the door shut and came on to stop between Duff and the transient eating at the end of the counter.

Mandy said uncertainly, 'Evening, Uncle Dan.'

Dan Ragan ignored the greeting and cut a glance at the stranger, handicapped by him. He said, 'Seen Frank?'

'Not tonight,' Mandy said. 'Why?'

'I been looking for him. Thought he might be here.'

'Well, I haven't seen him. Uncle Dan, you—remember Duff Doncaster. He and his folks were in the train, coming West.'

Ragan nodded, and that was all. He had learned what he said he had come in for, but he lingered, just standing there like a rock. The stranger was nearly through eating but seemed in no hurry. Without being asked,

Mandy brought coffee and put it before her uncle, trying to relieve the awkwardness of his silent waiting. Ragan ignored the coffee. A positive, unyielding, juggernaut of a man. Physically powerful, mentally rigid, spiritually frigid. Duff marveled at how sharply these qualities stood out now, with himself a grown man. Burley Loman, a living offense to the nostrils of a man like Ragan, had delighted in baiting him and the dignity of his office as captain of the wagon train. Burley had made a mistake there, but he had enjoyed making it.

The stranger finished eating, dropped a coin on the counter and left.

Mandy's face was pale. Ragan turned and put a long, at stare on Duff. 'It was Hob Loman I was looking for,' he said finally. 'You'll do. What's this about cattle and Pike Pelton fetching you here?'

'What did Mounts tell you?' Duff returned.

'I'm asking you.'

'And I'm asking what business it is of yours.'

Ragan fished into a pocket of his shirt. He brought out something that he dropped on the counter top. Duff stared at it, and so did Mandy. It was a whittling of soft pine wood. There was no mistaking what it was meant to be, all on one base—a miniature pair of wagons with their tongues reared up and lashed into a gallows frame. That was all, but it had a terrible meaning. It said even more to Duff than it had to Ragan. Hob couldn't be idle five minutes where there was a chunk of wood handy without pulling out his pocket knife.

Mandy looked sick. 'Where'd you get it?' she gasped.

'Somebody throwed it through my window,' Ragan said raggedly. 'Wrapped in paper around a rock. A while ago, right after Vince left. Till then, I thought he was seeing spooks.'

'Well, I never saw the thing before.' Duff's voice was shaky enough to make a liar of him. 'I have no idea what you do around here, let alone where you live. If Hob knew, it's news to me.'

'Easy enough to find out,' Ragan said. 'How long since you seen him?'

'Well,' Duff admitted, 'thirty-forty minutes.'

Ragan nodded, a hard, cold glint in his eyes. Duff glanced at Mandy, but she refused to look at him.

'I guess you've got a right to ask questions.' His voice was still unsteady. 'We've got cattle out on Cripple Creek we aim to winter and take to the mines. If we make out with 'em, we might settle here. But Pelton never fetched us, and I don't know why Mounts seen it that way and now you. Hob run into him in 'Frisco, and Pelton told him about the cattle trade up here. We'd made a silver strike in Nevada and had some money we wanted to put into something. And, as far as I know, that's it.'

'You were thick as thieves with him back

15

there,' Ragan said harshly. 'Since you're still running with him, you must feel like he seems to.'

'Up to a point,' Duff agreed, 'I feel like he does. Burley Loman never had a chance once he gave you an excuse to arrest and try him.'

'He got a fair trial, and it was a jury that found him guilty.'

'You sentenced him to hang.'

'I made the punishment fit the crime.'

There was no more uncertainty in Ragan about that now than there had ever been, Duff realized. A man with an open and shut mind who saw black and white and no gray at all. A man consternated by a fellow like Burley, who had lived wild and free, who had laughed as quickly as he fought. That had been plenty often, making him anathema in a train so constituted it had elected a bigot like Ragan its captain.

But all that was beside the point, Duff thought, staring at the tiny gallows. Nodding at it, he said, 'I don't know anything about that, Mandy. I hope you, at least, will believe it.' She refused to let him see what was in her eyes. He walked to the door and left.

He meant to get his horse and head for camp. But when he reached the livery barn, the hostler had a message from Hob. 'He come in to see if you'd left town,' the stablehand reported. 'Said to tell you to come over to Pelton's wagonyard. He scared up Pike.'

Duff said quickly, 'How long ago was that?'

'Just now.'

Duff's small hope vanished. It didn't prove that Hob hadn't been at Ragan's house. Yet if he had been looking for Pelton and finally found him—Duff shook his head. He was clutching at straws. Somebody was stirring up that old hornets' nest. It could only be Hob.

He and Hob had gone to the wagon yard as soon as they hit town, so Duff knew how to find it. It meant another walk along the long street, which had lost none of its activity, to a rocky flat against the river on the edge of town. The yard was a big, fenced enclosure that embraced several buildings. The open spaces were cluttered with wagons, parts, and all the other gear that went into a large freighting business. But the teamsters and stablehands were gone. The place was dark except for a lighted window in the building just inside the gate.

Hob and Pelton were in what must have been Pelton's office, although the room had the hodgepodge look of the yard outside. Duff would have known Pelton even if he hadn't expected to see him here. He had been a young man, then, and even in his middle thirties he looked much the same. He was a thin man, almost frail for the line of work he had chosen. Hob only gave Duff a quick grin, but Pelton climbed to his feet and offered his hand.

'So you're Duff,' he said, with a shake of the head. 'Wouldn't have known you. You stood high and skinny as a crane, the last time I seen you.'

'He still stands high,' Hob said. 'But he put on some meat. How come you stuck around, Duff? Sneak back to see if that Mandy was your little yellowhead?'

'She is,' Pelton said. 'Whether he sneaked back or didn't.'

Duff frowned and sat down in the roundback chair next to the one Hob was slouched in. Pelton returned to the swivel chair and lifted his feet onto the old desk. He looked relaxed and pleased with the occasion, and so did Hob. Duff wondered how long they had been together. He couldn't ask questions without having to answer some he didn't care to.

'I feel sorry for Mandy Fleeson,' Pelton went on. 'It's been the same old story for her out here in the so-called land of promise. Racking from post to pillar and back to post.' He shook his head. 'Girl that purty ought to have a man taking care of her instead of being stuck with those two miserable excuses.'

Hob said, 'Maybe Duff's gonna take care of that.'

Duff scowled. 'You mean she supports Fleeson and Mounts.'

'Oh, they work. But they both took to

18

boozin' out here. What they don't drink up of their wages, they're apt to lose bucking the tiger. It's Mandy gives 'em a home, on top of running her business. If it wasn't for the business, they'd have lean pickings some of the time.'

Hob said idly, 'They been here all along?'

Pelson shook his head. 'Oh, no. I stopped off here and went to work for the army. They all went down to the Willamette. Fleeson took land, but he didn't do any better on it than you'd expect of a man of his stripe. Mandy's ma died. That's when Frank took to boozin'. Then the gold rush started this town booming, and Ragan wanted to come back here. He don't like it, but Fleeson always hangs onto his shirttails and Mounts onto Fleeson's. The way they are now, they must gravel a hardshell like Ragan. But they're kin, and you got to hand it to Dan. He does his duty.'

Hob scowled, and Duff said quickly, 'Just how does Mounts fit in?'

'He's not a blood relation of Mandy's,' Pelton said. 'I bet she thanks the Lord for that every night. He was born to Frank's first wife by her first husband. But Frank raised him. They're two of a kind. Mandy's own ma was a sister of Ragan's wife. That makes her and Lois Ragan cousins.'

Again Hob frowned, and Duff said quickly, 'What kind of work do they do?'

'Frank works on the portage. Vince on the

19

docks. Dan's another who never done as well out here as he figured he was going to. Tried keeping store in the Willamette, then a grist mill. Up here he's a horse dealer, doing pretty well. Started a horse ranch he's building up fast as he can. Got a house in town and another out at the ranch. Lois keeps house for him and helps with his work. Still single, too. Mighty strange. She was a dark little beauty, back there. Time only added some mighty nice touches.'

Hob's eyes had gone hard and bright. He didn't need to be reminded what a striking girl Lois Ragan had been. Older than Mandy and about Hob's age, she had already been coming into womanhood. Being Mandy's cousin, the two of them were usually together. Being sidekicks, Duff and Hob were always together. So when the friendship sprang up between Duff and Mandy, it brought Hob and Lois together. It was all right with them, and before long they were paired off in a new way, Duff and Mandy, Hob and Lois.

To that point personalities hadn't begun to emerge in the wagon company and clash. Ragan was busy and might not have paid much attention to what his motherless daughter did during the long days. But once Burley started giving offense to Ragan, Ragan put his foot down hard. He wanted his daughter to have nothing to do with the son of such a man. Lois hadn't been like her father in that cold, self-certain way. She'd been a warm and human girl. But she was dominated by her iron-willed sire, and when he called a halt she obeyed . . .

As though wanting to hear no more about those people, Hob leaned forward in his chair. 'You said to come see you about places to winter,' he reminded Pelton. 'What's there to pick from?'

'Well, I wouldn't keep the critters on Cripple Creek,' Pelton said. 'It's empty country with plenty of grass, but it's high and cold in winter. There's a fine big prairie beyond them hills across the river. It's called the Klickitat. You'd be isolated. But if you wintered there you'd have a start for the Cariboo or Montana in the spring.'

Duff liked the sound of that. He would feel easier if the cattle kept them well away from Dalles City, at least most of the time. But he saw from Hob's expression and shake of the head that he had rejected it out of hand.

'East of here,' Pelton continued, 'there's country as good and a lot handier to town. Spring would find you setting better if you wanted to go into Idaho with your steers or to the Powder. But you'd have more competition in those camps.'

'Who's scared of that?' Hob asked.

Pelton liked that answer and grinned. He went on to describe the plateau between the Deschutes and John Day rivers. He called it get-through country. While large numbers

21

frequented it, they were nearly always on their way to someplace else. It began at the upper end of the steam portage, which terminated at the mouth of the Deschutes. It was crossed on its Columbia end by the old emigrant trail, which now was an improved stage and freight road to the country upriver. Running lengthwise of the rolling plateau was a similar road to the mining camps of the John Day. There were stage stations along both roads, some of them becoming settlements. The rest was pretty much the way its Creator had left it, a sweeping upland broken by hills and hollows, all covered by fine bunchgrass.

That didn't mean it wasn't being used by stockmen, Pelton said. They were just lost from sight in it. The first of them had brought their herds of cattle or horses across the mountains in the fall, turned them loose and come back in the spring to gather what winter had left to go on to the mine markets. Even now they were a vagrant breed, but they had come to realize the need to take care of the stock. So now they found a good location with a spring, built a corral near the spring, threw up a shelter for themselves and stayed with the stock. If they wanted to break the monotony, Dalles City was an easy ride. Other times they were where they could protect their investment from the inroads of weather, brute stupidity and predators.

Hob said eagerly, 'That's just the ticket.'

'Then I know the spot for you,' Pelton said with a smile. 'It's called Dutch Hollow, and it's only a fast two-hour ride from here.' He hesitated. 'But, if you see it as such, there could be a hitch. Dan Ragan's ranch is in the next hollow. In fact, it's the other half of Dutch Hollow. Different forks of the same crick.'

Hob's mouth dropped open. 'Don't he want both hollows?'

'Likely,' Pelton said dryly. 'But he's got nowhere near enough horses to lay claim to the empty one. And it don't belong to nobody till somebody puts it to use.'

Duff stared at him. In all that vast, empty country—yet it was the kind of insolence that would appeal to Hob. Shifting his weight in his chair, Hob said eagerly, 'You say they got a house out there?'

Pelton nodded. 'He's out there a lot. Lois even more. She takes care of things when Dan has to be gone. That too close for comfort?'

'I don't reckon they're the worry to us we are to them.'

'Good.' Pelton nodded his approval. 'Why don't you boys stay in town tonight, and we'll ride out there in the morning. I can spare a little time, right now.'

Hob cut a glance at Duff, who nodded his head. It made little difference, he thought glumly, where they wintered. As long as they were anywhere in the country, they would keep running into the past.

23

Having learned what he wanted from Pelton, Hob was ready to leave. Duff saw the restlessness building. Regardless of his easy ways, he had always to be on the move unless there was something important enough to hold him still. They talked only a moment longer, then left and went over to the Umatilla House. The place was crowded but there was a vacant third-floor room which they took.

Hob was quiet, but Duff didn't mean to leave it that way. As soon as they had shut the door of the room, he said, 'How long was it after you left me that you run into Pelton?'

'Not long.' Hob looked at him keenly, his eyes strange in the lamplight. 'Why?'

'I seen Dan Ragan. He was pretty upset.'

'I reckon he would be. He heard from Mounts.'

'There was more to it than that, Hob. Somebody heaved a rock through his window. There was a whittling with it. Neat job. Whoever made it is handy with a jackknife. It was supposed to be a gallows made of wagon tongues. Ragan come downtown looking for you. He run into me at Mandy's and talked to me, instead.'

Hob finished pulling his shirt over his head. 'He try to collect for the window glass?'

'It wasn't funny,' Duff snapped.

'No. But satisfying.'

'So you admit it.'

'All right. I never figured Ragan would give

24

me away like that.'

'How far's it going, Hob?'

'Far enough they'll wish they'd never been born.'

'Don't it make any difference that Lois is one of them?'

Hob's eyes went hard. 'Why should it? I know you never seen Mandy afterward. But I seen Lois. She told me Burley got what he had coming. I told her they'd live to wish they hadn't done it. She just laughed.'

CHAPTER THREE

Duff opened a sleepy eye, then the other, regretting the need to leave the first comfortable bed he had occupied in many weeks. Noises from a town already started on its new day reached his ears. Turning his head, he saw that Hob had left both the bed and the room. Duff sat up with a wide yawn and wiped the cobwebs off his face. The room was a pleasant one, well furnished. The proprietors proved their boast of running the most sumptuous hotel in the Pacific Northwest. He swept his long legs over the edge of the bed, rose and went to the window.

He found himself looking out over the river downstream from the hotel. The steamers had unloaded their freight in the night and were now taking aboard passengers for their runs downriver. A steam winch was hauling a small freight car up the incline from the landing to the main portage line at street level. Other cars were being loaded from the wharf boats. He wondered if one of the dockhands he saw was Vince Mounts.

That swept the last sleepiness from his mind, reminding of all that had happened the afternoon and evening before. Washing up and then hurrying into his clothes, he dwelt on the fact that Pike Pelton took the same satisfaction

Hob did in spooking those people. He wondered if Hob and Pelton were in cahoots in some kind of punitive scheme as a sideline to the cattle venture. Hob surely had reason, particularly if Lois had done what he said. But it didn't seem reasonable that Pelton would take the trouble. He hadn't been a friend of Burley's. Few in the wagon train had been by the time the explosion came. But Pelton was a little like Hob. That might have been why he stood up for Burley, even though Amos Bickle had been his wagon partner on that fateful journey west.

For all its promise of high adventure, the trail had a deadly monotony. Alkali blinded and choked and made eyes sore and nostrils red wounds. Camp fare became dismally tasteless. Wagon tires loosened on dished wheels. Sore-footed stock began to balk and quit. Trailside forage grew ever scarcer. So did fuel for the cook fires. If tempers were touchy to begin with, as Burley Loman's had been, they became explosive. Dislikes magnified, grudges deepened, fears mounted, and general human cussedness reached its peak.

There were a lot of sides to it, and to Burley. But the one that grew crucial was his quickness with his fists. He got into his first fight, over a campsite, while the company was still forming at Independence. He won it handily. The second came on the Blue as the outgrowth of an argument over a place in the line. By the time the wagons reached the mountains, he had licked two others. Yet he wasn't an overbearing man. His adversaries just hadn't got it through their heads that his were dangerous toes to step on. But the whole company recognized the danger by the time it came out of South Pass onto the hot, arid, grinding slopes of the Sandy and Green River.

Burley's last fight started over what, under less trying conditions, would have been little more than an annoyance. All that the others knew about it, later, came from what Burley said and what Frank Fleeson said in dispute. Amos Bickle hadn't been in shape afterward to say anything. The three had been on stock guard, for there had been Indian sign for several days. It was the rooster watch, daylight had come, and they were bringing the stock in to the train. Bickle surely hadn't intended what happened. He merely picked up a rock and shyed it at a lagging steer. The steer swung its head at the wrong moment, and the stone caught it square in the eye. Burley let out a roar and was on the man like a god of wrath.

According to Burley, Bickle pulled the knife before Burley hit him. Fleeson swore Bickle hadn't pulled it until he had to do so to save his life. One thing was sure. Bickle had slashed Burley bad enough to lay open the flesh over half a dozen ribs. Burley had taken the knife away from him and then beat him senseless. The man never regained

28

consciousness, and on the following night he died.

The outrage was enormous. Duff wouldn't bet whether it had forced Ragan to order Burley arrested and tried for murder or whether Ragan had grabbed the chance. Burley was a living refutation of everything Ragan believed and practiced with a certainty that was unshakable. Pike Pelton had been one of the few to see both sides of it, and Pelton had tried to defend Burley. He had pointed out at the trial that Burley, too, had acted in self-defense after Bickle pulled the knife, for Bickle would have killed him if he could. But Fleeson's inflamed testimony had cinched it. And Burley had undeniably gone on to beat the man more unmercifully than self-defense required. Pelton had conceded that but, it being a crime of unpremeditated passion, had asked for banishment from the train. Ragan waved that aside, and they hung Burley.

Duff understood pretty well what had gone into Burley's death. What he still didn't understand was what had gone into his life. Into making him a loner, a gusty, free-living man of violence who had died laughing at his judge, his jury and his hangman. He had been all over the South and Midwest, always on the move. So there were no kinfolks or even friends that Hob knew of. His son, then fifteen, had been cut adrift on the raw frontier with only a few willing to help him. Duff would

29

always be glad that, among these, had been his own parents . . .

With a shake of the head, Duff left the hotel room and descended to the lobby. He hadn't slept away too much of the morning, he discovered. The dining room was filled with people having their breakfast. He looked around for Hob without seeing him, then went out through the double front doors. The portage train waited on the street in front of the hotel. Passengers were going aboard to continue the journey into the interior.

Duff studied the train with interest. Its engine and cars were only about half the size of those back east. The freight cars had been loaded on the lower landing and drawn up by cable and a steam hoist. The passenger cars hooked behind were nearly full, with more people rushing out of the hotel or along the street to board. Even as he watched, the engine let loose a blast all out of proportion to its size. Like an echo, and not much louder, one of the steamboats sounded its own warning that it was about to depart.

And then Duff found himself staring with a fixedness that made him forget everything else.

He hadn't expected to recognize the man topping off the incline from the landing float. Maybe it was because he had known Mandy so well, and there was a family resemblance. Frank Fleeson showed the effect of the years, but this had only made his hair grayer and his face more lined. There was a man with him, and they both carried scoop shovels for some reason. The other man was saying something and laughing. Fleeson only looked glum and sour.

And then, as they strode by, Fleeson's gaze strayed Duff's way. His mouth opened, but he kept going, and the two went on to the locomotive. The other man tossed his shovel onto the cordwood stacked on the tender and climbed after it. Fleeson started to follow, then swung around and came tramping over to Duff. He still had the scoop on his shoulder. The knuckles of the hand gripping it were tight.

He stopped in front of Duff and said in a whiskey voice, 'Now, look here. It was a jury convicted Burley Loman. Not me, not Vince, and not Dan Ragan. Men picked from the company and scattered now all over Oregon and California. If you fellows have got a quarrel with somebody, go find them.'

Duff had once tried to like Frank Fleeson because he was Mandy's father. Now he found himself bristling. Not caring that it allied him with Hob in whatever Hob was there for, he said, 'Men picked by Dan Ragan. And not a one from the few willing to listen to both sides. Not a one who might have wondered from your colored testimony just how impartial a witness you were. Not a one who might have recommended the leniency Dan Ragan didn't want recommended. If there's a quarrel, Fleeson, I'd say it's with the men who stacked the deck.'

Fleeson swallowed. He seemed to be raking his mind for some better way to avert the wrath he so plainly feared. But at that moment a bell started to ring. The pony locomotive bucked forward, sending a noisy shudder along the train. Fleeson looked despairingly at Duff. Then he ran and caught the engine and swung up on the tender.

Duff stood watching the train glide off past the town along the edge of the river. Then he went back into the hotel and ate his breakfast. He had just returned to the lobby when Hob came down the stairs from the upper floors.

Hob said amiably, 'There you are. I went up to roll you out. Got your horse outside, and Pike's waiting. We'll go have our look at Dutch Hollow.'

Duff was more than willing to get out of town. The encounter with Fleeson had stirred things in himself, dangerous things he hadn't known were there. He said nothing about it to Hob. They went out. Pike Pelton sat his mount beyond the sidewalk, and the other horses were there. Pelton was smoking a cigar and seemed pleased with their excursion. He nodded to Duff, then the three of them rode up the long street together.

The wagon and stage road went east under a rock bluff that closed the pocket nestling town, fort and military reservation. Beyond this the land fell more steeply to the river, rocky, brushy and narrow. It was soon apparent why the portage was necessary. The river had narrowed noticeably, pushed in by prominences whose substructure had been bared by ancient floods and the grinding, still present wind. The channel itself was studded with rock islands so choking that the water surged and rolled and rushed. Wild as it looked, Duff saw Indians dipnetting from the rocks.

Pelton said Hudson's Bay Company trappers had called the islands *dalles.* That was supposed to mean stepping stones, and this had given Dalles City its name. There were other rapids on upriver, but the steamboats could run them. Yet the shores remained much the same up there. Rock everywhere, in heaps, pinnacles and long, high rims.

'Man starts here,' Hob said with a grin, 'he sure starts from bedrock.'

'He sure does,' Pelton agreed. 'And he stays at bedrock if he isn't just as hard as the country.'

'You seem to have done all right.'

'Yeah. I've done pretty well.'

Duff watched Hob with thoughtful eyes. He and Pelton had surely taken to each other. They seemed to understand one another without using many words. Duff had a feeling, almost, that he was being horned out. Pelton

33

was friendly, considerate, yet Hob obviously was his man. And Hob had revealed this unexpected, secretive side.

The road didn't change much for two or three miles east of town. Occasionally Duff saw stretches of the portage tracks below them, appearing and disappearing in the thick ground cover and winding away to the east. Then the road swung off from the river and threaded into a canyon. This route, Pelton said, was the one used when wagons had been the only connection between the middle and upper river steamboats. In the first days of the mining boom it had been littered from end to end with freight cast off from stuck or broken-down conveyances. Now all that shipping went on the steam cars.

The road wound through canyons, crossed creeks and climbed gradually toward the top of the wide headland that ran to the Deschutes River. The riders came to the first station east of the town to find the Canyon City stage there changing horses. The station was called Fifteen Mile for the creek that, at that point, came in from the south. But the road topped out on the benchland, shortly beyond there, and went on to the east. Not much later Pelton turned them along a pack trail that dropped off to the southeast.

'Shortcut,' he said. 'Road swings back from here to the upper landing. No use us riding all that way around.'

Not long afterward they came to a homestead and a crude toll bridge over the Deschutes, which wasn't a river that could be crossed at will. A short distance east of this they left the pack trail, which went on to join the road to the John Day mines. They were still on benchland, but a man lost sight of that in the vastness. Then they came all at once to the most attractive natural setting Duff had yet seen on their ride.

'That Dutch Hollow?' he asked.

'The south fork,' Pelton said. 'And yours for the taking.'

They were on a spiny ridge that fell to an immense natural meadow. A creek cut down the center, with groves of willow and cottonwood fringing it. This ran out of sight in either direction, and the distant side rose again to benchland. The day was clear enough so that when Duff turned in the saddle he could see the giant snow peak called Mount Hood. To the southeast ran mountains Pelton called the Blues. Eastward were the breaks of the lower John Day River.

Pelton was still looking into the hollow. 'Wild rye down there,' he said. 'Bunchgrass all over the benches. There's a spring in that biggest grove. I'd put my camp there so I wouldn't have to share my drinking water with the critters.'

Duff was completely taken by it. The bottom was sheltered, and in mild weather the steers could range up onto the benches. The groves would furnish firewood and poles for buildings and corrals. It would be easy to set up a sound, permanent headquarters, even.

Hob was interested in something else and said, 'Where's this so-called horse ranch of Ragan's?'

Pelton nodded northward. 'From this point, maybe two-three miles over there. But the hollows come together just before the crick empties into the Deschutes.'

'Reckon he'd put up a fight for this one?'

Pelton grinned. 'Scared he might?'

'Yeah. I'm shaking in my boots about that.'

Pelton nodded toward the bottom. 'Want to ride down?'

'Seen enough,' Hob said. 'It suits me fine. Duff?'

Duff remembered the way his hackles had raised when he confronted Frank Fleeson and what he had said. If he went along with this insolent move against Ragan, he would have declared himself in up to his ears on anything Hob wanted. Yet he said readily, 'Me, too.'

'Then let's go back by way of the upper landing,' Pelton suggested. 'They got a little hotel there where we can get a noon meal.'

It took only a comfortable, cross-country ride to bring them to the mouth of the Deschutes. This was a lush, shaded place with a large wooded island standing in the Columbia offshore. Just below the union of the two rivers, the Columbia swept into a bend, forced over by a staggeringly high rock cliff. Under this, nestled among the willows, was the main part of the settlement and, by the river, the landing for the upper river steamboats. Adjoining the portage installations were the yard and ways on which boatwrights had built the craft on that reach of the river. There was another, busier toll bridge over the Deschutes, a small store, and a wayside hotel.

The morning's upriver boat had left. But the train Duff had seen pull out of Dalles City was still there. The down-bound passengers loitered about while freight was being loaded onto the cars.

'They're late today,' Pelton said. 'Must have had trouble coming up through the dunes.'

'Dunes?' Hob asked.

Pelton explained. While the wagon road had been free to pick its way up the river, the railroad tracks had been confined to water grade. That hadn't been much of a problem when it came to building the fifteen-mile line. But between Five Mile Rapids and the Celilo. Falls there was a lot of sand. Since there was always a strong wind, this resulted in drifting along the track that even sand fences couldn't hold back. Duff understood why Frank Fleeson and the other man had carried scoop shovels when he saw them that morning.

They had a drink and then a hot meal at the hotel. Then they took a road that followed

37

back up the Deschutes for a short distance before lifting out of the gorge to the headland. The change, when they came out on top, was startling. It was all flat, grassy prairie up there, with no hint of the river. They had barely topped out when they saw, far forward, a daub of dust against the horizon.

Pelton kept watching this. Presently he said, 'Looks like a bunch of horses. It could be our friend making a delivery up the river.'

Duff cut a look at Hob, whose eyes gleamed instantly. Yet Hob didn't say anything, nor did Pelton add anything, and they kept riding forward. Presently it was obvious that the oncomers were two riders following about a dozen horses, all moving at a lazy trot. Pelton reined off the road, which was common courtesy when meeting loose animals for it cut down the chance of spooking them. Hob and Duff followed suit. The oncoming horses were a breed already becoming known as Oregons. They were larger than usual and made strong, fast riding and driving animals.

The bunch came nearer, then Pelton said, 'Dan's got his girl along.' He reined in, and there was a look in his eye that matched Hob's. 'So we'll be extra polite and stop to let 'em pass.'

Duff would have preferred to keep going, but with the others halted, he stopped. Sex had been indistinguishable except that one of the oncoming riders was smaller than the other, for they were dressed pretty much alike. But the smaller turned undeniably into a young woman. She was on the near side and seemed to pay no attention to the trio stopped at roadside.

But when Dan Ragan got close enough that the bunch didn't cut off his view, he straightened suddenly in the saddle. He said something. The girl flung a quick, startled look toward the three beside the road. Duff got his first good view of what was a dark and beautiful face. Lois Ragan had fulfilled the promise of her girlhood. Ragan spoke again, more sharply. But she tossed her head, swung her horse and came riding boldly toward the three watchers. Ragan reined in but didn't follow her. His face was set in the hard lines that, all through the years, Duff had associated with him.

Her own face didn't show much expression, but what there was wasn't friendly. She spoke in a flinty voice, her gaze raking the three of them, then settling on Pelton.

'What do you expect to gain,' she demanded, 'from bringing these men here?'

'Why, Miss Lois.' Pelton's voice was teasing. 'Why would I expect to gain something? They're friends of mine. Used to be friends of yours. Surely you haven't forgot.'

'I haven't forgotten it.' Lois looked at Hob again. 'Or the threat you made back there. I didn't think you meant it. Since you did, include me with the others.'

'Why, Miss Lois.' Hob's voice was even more mocking than Pelton's. 'What gave you the idea I ever included you out?'

She swung her mount, and the two of them rode on after the loose horses.

Pelton said admiringly, 'A mighty spunky young lady.'

'And that was a mighty odd question she asked,' Duff said. 'Mounts got a jolt, last night, when your name was mentioned. Ragan had the idea you brought us here. How come?'

'I stir up their consciences,' Pelton said easily. 'The same as you boys.'

'The girls had nothing to do with it'

'No, but they're kin.'

CHAPTER FOUR

Hob was shaving, standing in his undershirt with his galluses dangling at his thighs. He cocked his head and made the first razor stroke down his cheek, then stopped to regard the results. He was in a high good humor.

Without looking at Duff, he said, 'Better change your mind and come along. Stay off by yourself too long, and you'll go batty. A man's got to get the hell out of his system now and then.'

'I don't feel anything in my system,' Duff said, 'that I regard as hell.'

Hob stopped to wipe the razor, shaking his head. 'Don't know if I envy you or feel sorry.'

'Don't trouble to feel sorry. And if you figure to twist some tails again, you've done plenty already. You've had that bunch in a sweat now six weeks.'

Hob had shaved his cheeks and was working on his chin. 'Who said anything about them? I feel like a few drinks and a game, and I never did get to try that dance hall.'

'Have a go at it. And if you wind up in jail, I'll leave you there till you rot.'

'You would like hell,' Hob said easily.

That was all too true, Duff knew. No matter how far Hob went in the dangerous thing he had started, Duff kept finding himself going along at least passively. He resented Hob's taking advantage of that and drawing him into something that could be the ruin of both of them. The trouble was, way down deep, he felt a lot like Hob did. To tell the truth, he didn't mind having Ragan and Fleeson and Mounts sweat blood while they waited to learn what was in store for them. But spilling blood was something else, and it could happen if Hob got carried too far. So the best Duff could do was try to be a check-rein.

Hob gave up coaxing, finished his shave, then put on a clean shirt and a shoestring tie. He was exhilarated, as he always was with a lark ahead. He put on his best coat and hat. His care suggested that the dance hall and its easy-to-know girls were really in his thoughts.

'If you change your mind,' Hob said in parting, 'I'll put up at the Umatilla House. If I don't see you there, I'll be back in a day or so.' And then he was riding off down the hollow.

Duff went back into the dugout. October's cool brightness filled the sky. The first leaves were falling from the trees along Dutch Creek. It was early afternoon, and there was plenty of work to be done. Yet he didn't feel like starting anything. He didn't understand that. He wasn't inclined to go stale like Hob did and start itching for change and excitement.

Hob had earned his holiday. Within three days after their first look at Dutch Hollow, they had moved the herd and horses over from

42

Cripple Creek. They had paid off the farm boys from the Willamette they had hired to help drive and started digging in for winter. They had found a place by the creek with enough bank and slope for the dugout. That had been the first job, digging it out, providing drainage, a front wall of chinked poles and a roof of poles and earth. That was finished now, snug, warm and rainproof. They had packed out the essential furnishings, equipment and the winter supplies. They had built a pole corral with a shed for the horses they kept up for daily use.

Then, as always happened when there was nothing to hold him down, Hob got restless and started talking about a leisurely visit to town. Duff didn't understand why he, himself, dreaded going in for any other than business reasons. Mandy? He hadn't seen her during the several times they went in for supplies. Pelton? There was no denying that the man mystified and rubbed him the wrong way. Maybe that was jealousy. Pelton had probably been one of Hob's unmentioned reasons for wanting to go in.

Duff poured coffee from the pot kept hot on the stove that heated the dugout and sat down at the table. He wasn't much of a smoker except when he was nervous, and now he wanted a cigarette. He rolled it from the makings that lay on the table. But something kept boogering him, trying to make him admit

43

he should have gone with Hob. Pelton was certainly an influence, and it could be a bad influence if there was no one with Hob to try to counteract it.

Duff's gaze moved uneasily over the interior of the dugout. The two bunks built along the sidewalls. The glass windows they had brought out and put in the front wall. It was lavish for winter quarters and could well serve as a start on a permanent ranch. But, much as he liked the idea and the country, he had given up all thought of their staying in the country past spring. They would be lucky to get that far without Hob blowing them sky high. He had to do his best to keep that from happening. Once they had marketed, he would insist on going somewhere far removed from Dalles City. And from Mandy. That was why he didn't want to see her again. Or come near enough to be tempted to see her. And Pelton was the reason he should have overcome that and gone to town.

Duff shaved and changed his clothes, although he had no ambition to make a hit with the dance hall belles. When he was ready to leave, he was hardly more than an hour behind Hob. But that was long enough to keep him from catching up, so he wouldn't try.

He had saddled his horse when he saw the rider coming across the flat from the north. He knew instantly who it was and wanted to escape a confrontation, but that was out of the

44

question. So he waited by the corral gate, wondering what had induced Lois Ragan to ride over the bench from the north hollow.

He had ridden over, one day when Hob was busy elsewhere, for a look at the horse operation on the other fork of the creek. He had seen why Dan Ragan had started up there instead of picking the south fork. The rims over there were sharper, higher, and furnished a lot of ready-made fence.

Ragan had closed the few gaps with snake fences instead of a dugout, he had put up a nice house of milled lumber, well shaded by trees. There was a corral and barn and stacks of hay Ragan had cut or hired cut off the natural meadow. Duff had seen some of the horses. They were mares, and Ragan had a stud running with them he must have paid plenty for.

There was no question that Ragan had plans for all of Dutch Hollow. He couldn't help but know by now that the south fork had been occupied, but he had made no protest. He must be hoping what Duff did. That somehow the winter would pass without a tragic toll, and that spring would see the south hollow vacated.

Lois had seen and cut her horse toward. him. Duff liked the way she sat her horse and the sturdy erectness of her shoulders. There was no more friendliness in her face as she came up than there had been that day on the

Deschutes road.

She said without preamble, 'I happened to see Hob Loman heading for town alone. I thought maybe I could talk to you. You couldn't have found this place so soon without help from Pelton. That would be obvious, even if we hadn't seen you with him just before you moved in. Why? Bait? Do you hope to get my father so proddy he'll give you an excuse to kill him?'

Duff felt his cheeks grow hot. 'Dan Ragan may be a lot of things. But I don't think he's stupid enough to do that. Or know what makes you think we're low enough to try it.'

'You knew you were taking land he wants. When there was the whole outdoors to pick from.'

'For the winter,' Duff snapped.

'But does Hob Loman think that? And Pike Pelton?'

'Hob thinks that as far as I know. Pelton hasn't got a thing to do with it.'

Lois regarded him with thoughtful eyes. 'I hope not, Duff.'

She had used his first name. It suggested that she might have grown less certain of his own vengefulness. Without thinking, he said, 'Lois, why did you have to laugh at him, back there? If you hadn't, it wouldn't be like this. At least not as bad.'

She looked at him sharply. 'He told you about that?'

'Not till after we got here. I got a pretty strong feeling it was the big burr under the saddle.'

She seemed taken aback, as though she had never seen before that some of the responsibility rested on her own shoulders. 'I didn't realize—' she began in a small voice. She shook her head. 'He was saying those terrible things about my father and Uncle Frank and Vince. I had to tell him they only did their duty. Then he made those threats and—well, I laughed. I'm sorry I did.'

'How about telling *him* that?'

Her eyes narrowed. 'Not unless he proves himself a higher kind than his father. Which he isn't doing by a long shot.' She swung her horse and rode off.

When he left his horse at the Dalles City livery barn, shortly before dark, Duff learned that Hob's was there. Hob had taken a room at the Umatilla House but had gone out and hadn't returned. Sure that Hob would have gone to the wagon yard to see if Pelton was in town, Duff decided to check there.

Pelton was in his office, but he hadn't seen Hob. 'No sign of him.' His eyes sharpened. 'Something wrong?'

Realizing that he looked a little grim, Duff grinned weakly. 'He came in ahead of me, and I'm just trying to locate him. Didn't figure on coming, then changed my mind. If you see him tell him, will you?'

He turned to leave but Pelton stopped him with a wave of the hand. 'Set down.'

Duff took one of the roundback chairs. He had never talked with the man alone, and it was a chance to do so unhampered by Hob. He shook his head at the offer of a cigar and said bluntly, 'How come you stood up for Burley Loman when you were Amos Bickle's wagon partner?'

'Why—' Pelton looked startled. 'They were giving him a rough deal, that's all. He never meant to kill Bickle. He just flew off the handle when Bickle whammed a stone that hit that ox in the eye. Burley was good to animals and to his boy and to anybody that didn't gravel him. So when Bickle pulled a knife on him, he really seen red. He killed the man, sure enough. It called for punishment, if the train was to hold together. But hanging was pretty strong medicine.'

'But Bickle being your friend—'

'He wasn't,' Pelton cut in. I hit Independence on my lonesome and without an outfit for the crossing. Bickle was traveling alone. Talked him into taking me in his wagon, share alike on expenses and work. So we teamed up, but we weren't friends.'

'Did you know he carried a knife?'

'No, but I knew he was scared to death of Burley. I reckon he armed himself in case. The other men in the company were just about as scared. I liked Burley, myself, but I'd have thought twice before I crossed him. Say what you want, he was a lot of man.'

'You're a pretty persuasive man,' Duff said. 'But you didn't get very far with that bunch.'

'Felt like I was arguing with a Kansas cyclone,' Pelton said with a shake of the head. 'Jury and judge. Their minds were made up. They were scared of Burley. Any one of them might have been next, with no way to tell who it'd be. I'd even say they envied a man like he was. Scared of nobody and nothing on earth. Living the way that suited him and not giving a damn for their opinion. He was equal to that trail, and it had worn the rest of 'em down to bone and raw nerves. He was made for this country. He'd have done fine if he'd got here. So will Hob.' Pelton looked apologetic. 'You, too.'

'Thanks,' Duff drawled. He had been half of a mind to thresh out the hidden thing that seemed to lie between the Ragan-Fleeson families and Pelton himself. Maybe it was only what Pelton had once said it was. He had been privy to a chapter in their lives that he reminded them of every time they saw him. Duff got to his feet. 'If you see Hob before I do, tell him I'll be at the Umatilla House.'

'I'll do that.'

Duff found Hob in the Mount Hood, the most sumptuous of the town's many saloons. He was in a card game, with an impressive stack of chips on the table in front of him, and

49

very intent on the hand he was playing. Duff had a drink at the bar, then moved down to the side chairs and joined the gallery. Hob wasn't aware of anything except his own table. A man in a boat cap was dealing the cards. The game seemed to be plenty serious and fairly big.

Then Hob lifted his eyes, looked around and spotted Duff. He said something to the others, rose and came over. He looked surprised but pleased. He'd had some drinks, but you couldn't tell it without knowing him pretty well.

He said, 'Good. But they're running real sweet for me. I think I'll stick with it a while. Why don't you set in?'

'Reckon not,' Duff said. 'I'll get a bite of supper and wait at the hotel.'

Hob wrinkled his nose at such a tame pastime, then hurried back to the game.

Duff returned to the street. He felt better, for Hob was really caught up in his streak of luck. The game looked like one that could run well into the night, which had closed in fully. A string of freight wagons was tooling along the street. The evening stage from the east was drawn up in front of the Umatilla House. He moved idly along and then realized he had come up in front of Mandy's place of business.

She didn't serve full meals, yet she had all the customers she could handle. Beyond their heads and shoulders he could see her moving

50

about quickly. There was an older woman helping her. He stood there a long moment, then turned and moved down the street to another, full-scale eating house. It, too, was crowded, and he had to wait for a place to eat his supper. The cook was a man, but he knew his trade. Duff ate with relish. The talk around him was mostly about the mines at Buffalo Hump, where the latest excitement was. Maybe that would be a good place to head for in the spring. A killing there, like Hob dreamed of, then off to new parts. Never to see Mandy, even from a distance, again.

Relieved of immediate concern for Hob, Duff strolled the town to settle his supper. He was returning to the Umatilla House when, on down the street from the hotel, he saw Vince Mounts coming up from the steamboat landing. They were going to meet in spite of anything, so Duff shrugged his shoulders and kept walking.

Mounts was shuffling along with his eyes fixed on the plank underfooting. Then all at once he lifted his head and stopped dead in his tracks. They were still thirty feet apart, but Mounts only stood there, his mouth open while Duff came on toward him. Duff would have passed on in contempt, then he realized that Mounts meant to speak to him.

'Hey,' Mounts said. 'You got a minute?'

Duff stopped, surprised. There was a twist of harried concern on Mounts' face, a look almost of begging in his eyes. Duff said gruffly, 'What for?'

'I gotta talk to you.' Mounts looked around uneasily. 'But not here.'

'Anything you've got to say, you can say right here.'

'All right. Come on.'

Mounts followed Duff, who climbed the steps of the long hotel porch. 'Not through the lobby,' Mounts said hastily. 'This is all right. Over there.'

He nodded. Duff walked with him to the more remote of the chairs provided for loiterers. It was shadowed there, but Mounts looked around apprehensively before they sat down. Duff noticed the way the man's hands gripped the arms of his chair.

'All right,' Duff said.

'Well.' Mounts licked his lips. He was watching the street with bright, scared eyes. 'I figured that night, a while back, that you ain't as rambunctious as your partner. That maybe a man could talk to you. Not that it'll do any good, likely, but I figured—'

'Get to it,' Duff snapped.

'I'm trying. A man does something. Then the whole rest of his life goes sour. Figured if you knew—' Mounts faltered with a discouraged shake of the head. His face twisted, and he said with difficulty, 'What I'm trying to tell you is something I was told never to tell a soul. Figured if you knew, you could

52

get Hob Loman to take it into account and give a man a break.'

'Tell me and find out.'

'Well.' Mounts lowered his voice to a hoarse whisper. 'Maybe it wasn't the beating that Amos Bickle died of.'

Duff felt like he had been sledged. Something of terrible significance was worming its way out of the soul of Vince Mounts in the mortal fear that gripped him.

'Go on, Mounts.'

'If he didn't,' Mounts whispered, 'we ain't the ones to settle with. We only done our duty, the way things looked then. While—' His face sagged, and he said in despair, 'Oh, God.'

Pike Pelton was coming up the steps from the street, and Duff could see Mounts shrink in the chair. It looked like Pelton would cross the porch and go into the lobby. But he glanced their way, halted abruptly, then changed direction. He said, 'There you are,' to Duff and didn't seem aware of Mounts until Mounts sprang to his feet. Then Pelton added, 'Don't rush off, Vince.'

'Leaving, anyhow,' Mounts muttered.

He sidled the first few steps, then turned and hurried off.

Pelton said with a chuckle, 'Well. What got into him?'

Duff started to ask Pelton if he knew something about Bickle he hadn't told at the wagon yard, some illness, some enemy other

53

than Burley, if Burley could be called that. He kept silent. Mounts had tried to buy clemency for himself, maybe with a whopper of a lie. Duff decided to keep it to himself until he got another chance to talk to Mounts.

'Come over to see if you located Hob,' Pelton said. 'Find him?'

'Mount Hood. Tied up in a game.'

'Reckon I'll mosey over there. Come along?'

'Been there.'

Pelton nodded and went off up the street in the direction Mounts had taken.

CHAPTER FIVE

Vince was all but trotting when he reached the door of Mandy's place. Even so, he felt as cold as if winter already blew its icy breath down the river gorge. He had been a fool again. Maybe a bigger fool than when he tried, back there, to turn his secret knowledge into easy money. He opened Mandy's door hastily, stepped in and shut the door behind him. It didn't much help his feeling of being followed.

Her place was crowded. He had expected it to be, and that was the way he wanted it. She didn't notice him, nor did Ellie Watts, when he slid on into the back room. Mandy did her short-order cooking out front, and there was nothing in the back room but supplies and a couple of work tables. But a lamp burned there. No shadows. All bright and warm and, momentarily, safe.

But not as private as he would have liked. Mandy had seen him, after all, and came back looking uneasily curious. She said irritably, 'What are you doing here?'

'Nothing,' Vince said innocently. 'Just dropped in.'

'You're scared spitless. They in town again?'

'What they?'

'You know who I mean.'

'Seen Duff.'

'He jump you?'

'I just seen him.'

Mandy shrugged and hurried back to her work.

Vince's eyes slid to the drawer in one of the old backroom tables. He edged over and quietly opened the drawer. Mandy's stingy gun was there, a little double-barreled Remington. He checked to make sure it was loaded. She had put it there long before that pair of hellions showed up in the country. Rough customers sometimes got out of hand with her or Ellie, for there weren't half enough women in Dalles City to go around. Vince slipped the gun into his pocket. He felt better. He had rushed in to get it after the first time he saw Hob Loman. But Ellie had been working in the back, that time, so he hadn't been able to take it.

He left by way of the back door and walked along the alley to a side street. He wished he knew where Frank was, for Frank was his only real confidant. Dan Ragan had little use for him, and Lois despised him as much as Mandy did. But ever since those two hard cases showed up, Frank had been avoiding him. It was as though even Frank was abandoning him to his fate.

Feeling very lonely, Vince moved along a back street long familiar because it led eventually to the tall, narrow house where he lived with Frank and Mandy. He kept his hand on the stingy gun. Even in the friendlier surroundings he kept getting a feeling that somebody was following him. He walked faster and faster and came to the narrow footbridge over the creek. He walked it carefully in the darkness, for there was only one handrail. Mandy swore that some night Frank or he would come home tighter than ticks and drown themselves.

The house was beyond the bridge. It was surrounded by brush and big rocks but was the best they had been able to afford in a town where building lots came high. He reached the house, hurried inside and shut the door. He wanted to light every lamp in the house. But if the place stayed dark, anybody investigating it would think nobody was home or everybody was there and in bed. He made his way through the darkness to his own room, which was a lean-to off the kitchen.

The bottle was up on the partition plate in the unfinished room. He and Frank had to keep their private stock out of Mandy's sight and reach if they didn't want it dumped in the sink. He had a couple more hidden bottles, but all he wanted now was to settle his nerves. Then maybe he could take the stingy gun and do what he had to do if he wanted to live.

He pulled the cork from the bottle with his teeth. It was harder that way, but he had seen a transient open a bottle like that one time. It had made the fellow look fiercer than he had looked already. Vince knew he'd likely never look fierce enough to scare anybody, himself. But he could feel fierce, sometimes. There was no trick way to achieve it, though. To really get the feeling, to be aroused and carried away by it, he had to be with people who felt fierce, themselves. Then he could even outdo them.

He took a long pull on the bottle, shuddered and thought about the one real high moment in his defeated life. The feeling that had gripped the wagon company had started when Frank and Loman fetched the man Bickle in from stock guard, bloody, and as limp as a sack of corn. But until the next morning it had been *just* another case of somebody getting on Loman's wrong side. Then word went around the camp ground that Bickle had died in the night in his wagon.

Vince took another pull on the bottle and felt the liquor land in his stomach. For years it had been a tonic to him to think about that day and the feeling that had charged the wagon company and united it in hatred and fear of Burley Loman. The man had proved himself a maniac, a menace to them all, and finally he had laid himself wide open. Even Vince had found himself denouncing Leman and demanding that he be brought to time.

There had been one bad period in that day, coming when, to everybody's surprise, the dead man's wagon partner rose in defense of Loman. Everyone had been scared Dan Ragan would heed Pelton's plea for banishment. Frank most of all. Banishment wouldn't keep Loman from sneaking back and. dealing with the man who testified against him. Testimony Loman said was twisted and prejudiced, as maybe it had been. Frank had known that Dan Ragan had come to detest Loman. And Frank never missed a chance to curry favor with Dan.

But Vince didn't think Frank's fear was why Ragan disregarded Pelton's plea. Had Dan been an ordinary man, he might not have minded an opportunity to get rid of a shiftless, shirt-tail in-law. But Dan wasn't ordinary. He was a set man, and what Loman had done, everything that Loman was, his whole record and character had been on trial in Dan's hard mind. In his lights it called for punishment just as hard. The sentence had been the only one possible to Dan.

Pronounced, it had brought on the biggest moment Vince had ever lived. The sentence was so popular there had been plenty of help making a gallows by rearing two wagon tongues in the air. They brought up a horse for the convicted man to mount. Maybe it was Loman's grin that froze things, his look of contempt while everybody waited for somebody else to take the final steps.

Something had come over Vince then that he had never felt before. He stepped right up and tied the rope for them. He had never tied a hangman's knot, and it wasn't a very good one. After Loman mounted the horse and Vince had larruped it from under him, he had threshed a long time. But, good job or clumsy, Vince Mounts had done what no other man there had dared to.

If only it hadn't turned out that they might have hung the wrong man.

That was the pure misery of it. They just could have, although it had become more likely when Hob Loman and his sidekick showed up under the wing of Pike Pelton. So it had been crazy to think he could have made Duff believe it, let alone Hob. As stupid as letting it slip to Pelton, back there, that others had learned of the big chunk of money Amos Bickle had had in his wagon, unknown to the company but maybe not to his wagon partner. Vince shook his head, wondering what had made him think he could scare a man like Pelton out of some easy money. It had paid off in nothing but grief. Pelton had laughed at him and, scared, Vince had told Frank what he had done. Equally scared, Frank told Dan. Vince had got the lacing down of his life, but they still had nothing but suspicions about Pelton until Hob arrived.

So now Vince knew he had to kill Hob or be killed, and maybe to keep the others from being killed, too. For Pelton wouldn't kill him or them, himself. If he were willing to risk that, he wouldn't have waited so long. What a strike he must have thought it when he stumbled into

Hob in San Francisco and saw his killer ready made. Like when he saw his chance, back there, to get Bickle out of the way and grab his money . . .

Vince took another pull on the bottle, corked and hid it again. He hadn't drawn any courage from it. Instead, it had made him unsteady. He pulled the stingy gun out of his pocket and stood in the darkness getting his hand used to it. He was sure that if Duff was in town, so was Hob. He would have to lay for Hob, shoot from hiding and trust to luck.

Vince was still there, reluctant to return to the town, when he heard the noise on the front porch. He had a wild, thumping moment before he realized it was only Frank. Vince didn't want to see him. He had to go back downtown and get it settled. He slid out into the dark kitchen to make for the back door just as a match was struck in the sitting room. The hunger for sympathetic company, even for light, was too strong. He turned and went into the other room. Frank put the chimney back on the lamp he had lighted and looked at him. He belched and stood swaying. He had taken on an even bigger load than Vince had.

'Didn't know you were home,' Frank said thickly. 'What you setting in the dark for? Or do you wear that hat and coat to bed?'

He was in a mean mood. That was bad, but Vince knew he had to talk. 'I done it again, Frank,' he said miserably. 'I was starting to tell

Duff Doncaster about the letter Dan got from back East. About Bickle's money. And along come Felton. The look he give me was pure poison.'

'You muttonhead.' Frank regarded him with bitter eyes. 'You just can't leave bad enough alone.'

'Well, if Hob knew he was being used for a killer by somebody he trusts—and that he might wind up the goat even if he don't kill anybody, the way we think Burley did—'

'He'd still be after us,' Frank cut in testily. 'His old man's as dead innocent as he'd be dead guilty.'

Vince knew that it was true. There was no escaping what he had to do.

Frank said, 'Leave the lamp burning for Mandy,' and went off into his bedroom. Vince left the house.

The night was still lonely, and it was silent save for the creek and the low, far sounds of the town. Vince reached the footbridge and almost turned back. It was then that he saw the figure, stepping out at him from behind the big rock. He sobbed, 'No!' and tried to get his hand into his pocket, sure that if he turned away from the advancing shape he would get a knife or a bullet in his back. He tried to yell for Frank, but terror froze his voice box. The damned gun was fouled in the worn lining of his pocket. He wheeled to run and felt hands close on his neck. He almost got out a yell before it was blocked off. He heard heavy breathing that wasn't his own, then a soft, laughing voice.

'Vince? You know how a hung man dies?'

Vince clawed at the hard, brown hands that had closed like a vice on his throat. He kicked and struggled and tried to fight, but it did no good. The hands held tight. He couldn't even get turned around to face his fate.

'He suffocates,' the voice went on. 'His lungs heave and buck and buck and heave till he chokes. That's why he's lucky if his neck breaks. He still chokes, but it's faster.'

Vince's arms were lead weights at his sides. His head spun and crazy lights danced in his eyes. He was tired and discouraged, and it didn't seem to him there was much point in fighting. In living.

'So we won't bust your neck, Vince, and let it take longer. That way you'll be breathing when you slip off that bridge into the crick. Gotta have water in your lungs. Poor Vince. Damn fool trying to walk that bridge in the dark dead drunk. You're gonna be important again, Vince. Whole town'll be talking about you, tomorrow . . .'

He threshed helplessly, hearing the voice, knowing how a hung man went, feeling the buck and heave of his dying lungs.

CHAPTER SIX

Far out on the river Duff could see the lights of the steam ferry that shuttled between the sandy shore at townside and the landing under the rock bluff to Washington. A man would suppose that, this deep in the night, the ferry would be tied up, as were the two steamers winking their standing lights near where he stood. The fact that the ferry still ran showed what a restless, on the move country it was.

The more he saw of this locality, the more he liked it. He wasn't like Hob, who tired of a place as soon as he had wearied of its excitements and pleasures. When he, himself, found a place he liked, he grew ever more interested in it in all its aspects. This was such a place. He wished it hadn't been spoiled for them, even before they ever laid eyes on it.

He had followed a road for a little ways west of the town, killing time. And feeling uneasy. He had sat on the hotel porch for an hour or more, after that queer approach by Vince Mounts. Persuading himself that the scared little man had been trying for protection by confusing the matter of how Amos Bickle had really died. It had been a useless try, at best. Not only Bickle but Burley Loman had died, were dead, would always be dead. There was no cloudy issue about Burley's death, or about

64

who had been the judge and the witness and the hangman.

Duff turned on the dark road and walked back to the edge of town, headed for the Umatilla House to turn in. He had lost track of Hob completely, which wasn't strange in a town so crowded they could have missed each other narrowly more than once. All he knew for sure was that the poker game in the Mount Hood had broken up by the time he finally went back there to check on Hob. Maybe the game had been transferred to some more private place. When the gambling fever was up in Hob, he could stick all night. Or maybe he had found a better guzzling and girling companion in one of the other players than his usual sidekick was. One of several other things, maybe, including the thing that kept Duff uneasy. The only certainty was that he hadn't found Hob in any of the other saloons or at the dance hall.

By the time he came to the hotel steps, Duff had decided on one more look at the public places along the street. He went on and with no better results than he had before. He decided that it didn't mean a thing. Hob had forgotten his promise to meet, as soon as he had left the game. It had happened in other places, at other times.

And then Duff found himself standing across from Mandy's place. He glanced guardedly toward it exactly when she came to the front window, reached up and drew the shade. That brief glimpse of her, and then a checked breath while her silhouette dissolved on the blind. He stood there for a long moment before the light inside went out. He was sure, then, that she was closing up for the night.

He went across the street and came up behind her. She was turning the key in the lock of the door. She withdrew the key and put it in her purse before she turned. She straightened and gasped.

'Oh!'

'Mandy,' he chided. 'It's me.'

'I didn't know that.' He had surely rattled her, though. She tried to smile and added, 'You hungry? I always lock up about this time of night.'

'I was going to ask to walk you home. But not if you're *that* spooked of me.'

'I'm not spooked of you at all.' That wasn't so. She had nearly jumped out of her shoes when she saw him. 'But I got to thinking you were spooked of me. What changed your mind, tonight?'

'I didn't change it. I just haven't had a chance to see you till now.'

'You've been in town several times,' she contradicted. 'I decided you classify me with my father and Vince Mounts. Cut me in with the culls, the way you see it.'

'I'd have as much right to do that,' Duff

retorted, 'as you have to cut me in with Hob. At least, with what you think he come here for.'

'You've got more right.' Mandy looked down at the sidewalk. 'I know my family is trash. What they are I am, I guess.'

'What they are, you're not,' he snapped.

She looked up again. He saw she had hoped he would say that. 'And what Hob is, you're not,' she said. 'He's not trash, but he's a bronco like Burley Loman.'

She hadn't consented to his escorting her home. They simply started walking along together. Just as in the days long past, she took two steps to his one. A light, smooth, girl walk that had always pleased him. He thought about her calling Hob bronco. It fit him. But a bronco and a killer horse were two different things.

'No matter what you say,' Mandy resumed. 'You're worried about Hob's intentions.'

'So are you and Lois. You seem to think he'd wipe out the lot of you.'

'He's got hate enough to cover everybody,' Mandy said.

'And even kill women?'

'He's not entirely sane, Duff. I wish you'd keep that in mind.'

They reached the end of a rickety sidewalk and followed on along a dark and wretched road. Then all at once Mandy stopped and looked at him. They had come to a spindling footbridge over a creek. There was a house in the cramped pocket on the far side. A couple of its windows showed lamplight.

'I live over there,' she said quietly. 'This is as far as you better come.'

He wasn't afraid of Fleeson and Mounts put together. Or of their knowing he had walked Mandy home. But if she didn't want him to see her to her door, it was all right with him. Yet he hadn't come within a mile of taking up where they had left off, back there.

'Well, then. Goodnight,' he said.

'Goodnight. Oh, Duff!'

He hadn't planned to do what he did. But he hadn't expected her to look at him with so much feeling in her face. She didn't resist when he put his hands on her sides. Or when they slid on and his arms came around her and wrapped tight. Back on the crossing they had once kissed, shyly, out of curiosity. But with nothing like the surge of feeling that swept over them now. He felt her slim, firm body yield itself, and her mouth gave itself to an urgent seeking of his.

All at once she pushed back, completely free of him, and said unevenly, 'We'll be sorry we did that.' She turned and fled.

He couldn't believe that he would be sorry or would ever permit her to be.

Hob was in the hotel room when Duff reached it. He hadn't been there long, for he was partly undressed for bed. He had been drinking but hadn't reached the point of drunkenness. He had found his good time. The restlessness in his eyes had given way to the lazy good nature that showed his real self.

'What did you scare up for yourself?' Hob asked amiably. 'Thought I'd come home and find you dead to the world.'

It was none of Hob's business, with him being so secretive about his own affairs. 'I didn't scare up anything,' Duff said grumpily. 'What happened to you?'

'That's something a gent never tells.'

Hob gave him an owlish grin. He crawled into bed and drew the covers over his ears.

Duff undressed, blew out the lamp, and went over to the window. It looked out over the town. Off there somewhere, lost in the night, was Mandy's house. He wondered if their long kiss still tingled on her lips as it did on his. He wondered if she had recognized his desire for her and let it kindle a desire for him. They were man and woman, now. This new thing had come to enrich what they had had before.

He felt guilty but not about that. Returning to the hotel, he had decided to give Hob a choice. They would move on to some other winter range together, well away from here. Or they would split the herd and he would move on alone and free his hands to do what he really wanted.

Yet the minute he stepped into the room he

had known he lacked the courage to gamble himself, and Hob's feeling of close friendship for him, against what Hob felt for his enemies. So he stood now looking over the roof and treetops of the benighted town, trying to find comfort in Hob's looking relaxed and at peace with the world again.

What Hob had said implied that he had scored with a dance hall girl. That would explain his being impossible to find that evening. He hoped this was the case. Something like that might be enough to keep him reined in.

Duff was the first to wake up to the new day, helped by his having set his mind to it before he went to sleep. He had decided to go back to camp, regardless of whether Hob was ready. He didn't want to eat breakfast with Hob in the hotel dining room. He slipped out of bed, washed, shaved and dressed, managing not to wake Hob up. He slipped out of the room and went down to the usual busy scene on the streets.

Mandy's place was open and had been for some time. But the trade had thinned out. Most of those she served breakfast to had been up early to catch the portage train or the stage or some other conveyance that would take them on somewhere else. The woman who helped her was there, too, working at the stove while Mandy waited on the counter. Mandy didn't notice him when he took one of the vacant places. He thought she looked grim. He wondered if she regretted already what had happened between them the night before. He glanced over the breakfast menu, chalked on a blackboard on the wall.

Then she came up to him, and seeing him didn't lighten her eyes. But she did acknowledge him with a slight change in her eyes, and with a rather short, 'Good morning. What are you having?'

'Saddle blankets and coffee,' Duff said, puzzled about it.

She called the order to the woman cook. She hesitated, turned back and said in a lowered voice, 'Do you know where Hob Loman was, last night?'

Duff thought he had a pretty fair idea, but it wasn't something he could explain to Mandy. 'He was in the room when I got there. Why?'

'Vince didn't come home last night. I'd think he was laying drunk, somewhere, but I've got a little hand gun I keep here. I looked this morning, and it's missing. He was in here, last night, and my father talked to him right after that. Then Vince left the house and never came back.'

'Maybe he lit a shuck, Mandy. Boogered out.'

She shook her head stubbornly. 'He wouldn't leave Frank, especially when he's so scared. He'll show up, I suppose. But with Hob in town, it worries me.'

71

Duff's spirits hit bottom. Always that. He didn't give a damn about Vince Mounts. He resented him for the part he had played back there and was still playing here. He didn't care what happened to him but he sure as hell cared how it happened. He remembered the satisfaction on Hob's face, the night before. There were ways for a man to obtain it without a woman. He thought of the scared little man on the hotel porch, trying to win clemency with a whopper. Maybe Mounts had seen something coming with sharper eyes than Duff Doncaster's.

Mandy brought his coffee and, a moment later, his griddle cakes. He avoided looking at her eyes. He was boogering, too, because of the potentialities. If something had happened, she had been right when she said, 'We'll be sorry we did that.' She went on with her work. He ate his breakfast, paid for it and left.

He was at the livery barn to get his horse when he changed his mind and went back to the hotel room. He entered noisily enough to wake Hob, who sat up in bed. Hob stared at him but changed his mind about protesting the noise.

Standing in front of him, Duff said heavily, 'Did you threaten Vince Mounts again?'

'Didn't even see the worm,' Hob said innocently. 'Why?'

'I ate breakfast at Mandy's, and she's worried about him. Seems he didn't come

72

home last night. He was in her place, and this morning she discovered a gun she kept missing.'

'What do you know?' Hob grinned. 'Vince hit for yonder.'

'What're you up to? Trying to scare 'em all out of the country?'

'I'm not scaring 'em,' Hob said. 'They're scaring themselves.'

Duff couldn't be sure whether the gleam in Hob's eyes came from surprise or satisfaction. Even so, Duff felt relieved. It was a way he hadn't thought of, himself, for Hob to gain a bloodless victory. If Mounts didn't turn out to have been dead drunk on some back lot, he might well have decided on a change of surroundings. It wasn't hard to conceive of Fleeson's nerve breaking, also, and his deciding to go elsewhere for his health. Mandy would be better off rid of the pair. Ragan might be something else again, yet he had taken the loss of half of Dutch Hollow without a protest. He surely wasn't hunting trouble, whether or not he would run from it.

'I'm heading back to camp,' Duff said, trying to dismiss it. 'You ready?'

Hob thought a moment, then nodded. 'I guess so. Why don't you bring the horses around while I get set?'

Duff went back down to the street. He was in no hurry, for he could get the horses faster than Hob could dress and eat breakfast. So he let himself be drawn up the street a couple of blocks, to where a knot of men had gathered. There seemed to be some kind of excitement there. He was a half-block short of the group when he saw Pike Pelton peel off from its edge and come walking toward him. Duff would have passed him with no more than a greeting, but Pelton stopped him.

'Wait a minute, Duff. I been wondering why you were hobnobbing with Vince Mounts, last night on the hotel porch.'

Duff studied him. It was a natural question for at the very least, he wouldn't cultivate Mounts' company. 'It was his idea, not mine. He was trying to sell me a bill of goods when you come along and scared him away.'

'What kind of a bill of goods?'

'He didn't get far enough for it to make sense. Something about if the truth came out, Hob might feel different. I took it for a sandy. What made you curious?'

'They just brought him in.' Pelton nodded to the group up the street. 'To the funeral parlor, up there.'

Duff felt like he had been sledged. 'Mounts?'

'Himself.' Pelton grinned. 'Frank found him this morning in the crick that runs by his house. Maybe it'll convince Frank to put another rail on that bridge before he goes off, himself, some night when *he* comes home with a snootful.'

Duff remembered the bridge. Mandy had run across it safely in the dark, the night before, but she had been sober, not blind, staggering drunk. Pelton had already dismissed the matter. So would the town, for Mounts had been a no-account. But Duff didn't find it that easy to get it out of his own mind.

CHAPTER SEVEN

They were turning off up Fifteen Mile when Hob said, 'What's eating on you? Haven't heard a word out of you since we left town.'

Duff kept his eyes on the wagon road ahead. He hadn't been able to broach Hob about Mounts. He had been waiting with the horses when Hob came out of the hotel, and they had headed out at once. But they had to talk about it. It would bedevil him until they did.

He said, 'Can you prove where you were, last night? I mean from the time you left the game and when I found you in the room.'

Hob looked at him with sharp eyes. 'Why should I prove it?'

'You might have to.'

'Why?'

'Mounts is in the funeral parlor. I learned it just before we left.'

'Well, what do you know?'

'Good news, is it?'

'I don't feel tearful.' Hob shook his head. 'How come. Did he use that gun you said he swiped from Mandy on himself?'

'He drowned.' Duff repeated what Felton had told him. 'The only ones who'll doubt that are the Fleesons and the Ragan.'

'And maybe you.'

'It won't be a joke,' Duff snapped, 'if they go

76

to the law. You made threats to Lois at Fort Hall. She remembers them. You pulled that lunatic stunt with the wood carving on Ragan, when we first got here.'

'So even you think I pushed Vince in the crick?'

'I suppose he fell off the bridge,' Duff snapped. 'But I'd feel better if you could prove where you were at the time, in case somebody asks who's got a star on his chest.'

'I was in the Mount Hood, then the hotel room.'

'Between times?'

Hob scowled. He had never liked questions. He disliked that one in particular. But he seemed to agree that the law wouldn't be easily put off, if he had to explain. After a moment, he said, 'All right. I was with a woman.'

'I figured so. Well, gent or no gent, you might need her.'

'That would be too bad. She left on this morning's boat downriver.'

Duff said with a snort, 'Real gallant. You'd hang before you'd sully her good name. Or do you know her name?'

'Sure. Ruby.'

'Ruby what?'

'That's all the name she ever gave me.' Hob's face was stubborn. 'She summered in Lewiston and didn't want to get snowed in there for the whole winter.'

'Where was she heading?'

'She wasn't sure. Some place warmer than them mountains, she said.'

'How'd you get hold of her last night?'

Hob said testily, 'Now, look here—'

'Damn you!' Duff's glare took the truculence out of Hob. 'I'm asking questions you might be asked by nightfall. Your answers are squirmier than snake tracks.'

Hob said doggedly, 'They're true. I knew her in Virginia City a year or two back. You would have, too, if you weren't so straight-laced. She was a big hit with the fellas. After I left the game, last night, I run into her on the street. She let me come to her room in the Washington, and that's the size of it. Satisfied?'

'Sure,' Duff said. 'You sound real convincing.'

They reached Dutch Hollow close to noon. After their hot exchange, it had been a silent ride. Then, when they reached the high ground from which Pelton had first shown them the south fork, Hob threw it off. He reined in there, causing Duff to stop, also.

'Damn but that's a sight down there,' Hob said. 'Your towns are fine when a man's feeling his oats. But most of the time you can give me a big, beautiful piece of country like this. Nobody in it but me and you.'

Maybe it was a diversion, but that made good listening. Duff couldn't help take hold of it, for that was the way he felt himself.

Carried away in spite of his pessimism, he

said, 'We could hold back the young she stuff for brood stock, next spring, and still make money in the mines. Then we could go back to the valley for some bulls and let nature take her course.'

Hob nodded agreeably. 'At the same time we bought bulls, we could pick up more beef stuff to winter. By the time the mines played out, we'd have us a going ranch and money behind it.'

'It's something to think about.' Duff was afraid to show too much interest.

'Yeah.'

Hob seemed really to mean it.

They rode on again. They nooned at the camp and, afterward, checked on the cattle and found everything in good shape. Nobody came out from town that day to ask Hob questions, nor the next day and the day after. For some reason, Ragan and Fleeson weren't seeking the protection of the law for themselves by supplying the sheriff with a motive for Mounts' death and a suspect. If they found it advisable to let the death go as an accident, Duff guessed that he should, also.

Hob seemed to have gotten the hell out of his system again until one morning while they were eating breakfast. He said without warning, 'I had a look at the north fork, yesterday. You ever been there?'

'I had a quick look at it once,' Duff admitted warily. 'There's the place for a ranch

79

headquarters. Better than this.'

Duff felt the frost gathering again on his backbone. 'I reckon that's why Ragan picked that fork for it.'

Hob laughed. 'Must aim to live there sometime, him and Lois. House, barn, corrals, everything first class. Damned if I don't envy them.'

'Covet, you mean.' Duff pushed back his chair. 'Get this straight, Hob. Try grabbing the north fork, too, and you and me bust up.'

Hob looked surprised. 'Who said anything about grabbing? Ragan might be happy to sell out. Figuring there ain't room for him and us both in Dutch Hollow.'

'He knows that, all right.'

'He will by spring, anyhow. And we'll have the money to buy him out when we get back from the mines.'

That was as close as they came to admitting that they were talking about a freeze out and land grab. But this was a highly unusual case, which kept Duff from rejecting it out of hand. Hob had to have satisfaction. It would be so much better to gain it bloodlessly. And if Dan Ragan was spineless enough to let himself be forced clear out of Dutch Hollow because of his fears, he would deserve to be forced clear out.

'If Ragan was really willing to sell,' he conceded. 'And if we paid a decent price for his rights and improvements, I'd go along with it. I mean if it's the fear he already feels that makes up his mind for him. You do one damned little thing to add to that fear, and I'm out of it and we break up. Understand?'

'I heard you.'

That didn't actually agree to a thing.

Duff did his share of the day's riding thinking about the fear Hob seemed to be using as his weapon and almost convincing himself that this was all Hob had in mind. It was a potent weapon, especially if it was mixed with guilt. Men laboring under such an uneasiness even became superstitious. 'A man does something,' Mounts had said, that evening on the hotel porch, 'and the rest of his life goes sour.'

Other things Mounts had said that evening came to mind. Like that he knew something he had been told never to reveal which might make Hob more merciful. Something beclouding the way Amos Bickle actually died. Mounts might not have been making that up. If not, Burley Loman could have been framed. But it was hard to believe that Dan Ragan might have done so. Fleeson might have, or Mounts. But there would have been nothing for Ragan to gain. It would be wholly unlike him to bend his self-righteousness to protect one of the others or somebody else in the wagon company.

But if those three knew they had hung an innocent man, if not knowing beforehand then learning it afterward, they would surely have guilt mixed with their fears. It would be no wonder that Hob's arrival in the country had scared them spitless. Even if the girls didn't share the guilt, and Duff was certain that Mandy didn't, their fathers would fear for them, too. For the daughters could be a means, themselves, of punishing their sires.

It was only two days later when Duff rode in from his morning work to see half a dozen loose horses in the pole corral he and Hob had built. He was suspicious even before he saw the R brand they wore. Hob was indoors, fixing their noon meat. There was a tattletale excitement in his eyes.

Duff said without greeting, 'Where did you get the Ragan horses?'

'Strays,' Hob said. 'I picked 'em up at Stony Ridge Spring.'

'You should have shooed 'em home. Why corral 'em?'

'They're impounded.'

'Come off it.'

Hob's face set. 'If Ragan figures to graze horses on our grass, he can pay for the grass.'

'Ragan's never admitted our right to this fork. You know that.'.

'Then it's time he admitted it.'

The stubbornness in Hob's face warned Duff not to bring up his threat to pull out if Hob made deliberate trouble. But he said angrily, 'We're taking 'em over the plateau and turning 'em loose on the other fork, and that'll be the size of it.'

'The hell it will.' Hob ladled stew from. the pot he had heated up. He put the dishes on the table. 'I don't know how long they mooched on us. But from here on it's costing Ragan a dollar a head a day.'

'He won't even miss them for a long while.'

'Then he'll run up a big feed bill.'

'I'll have nothing to do with a thing like that.'

'You won't need to.' Hob grinned. 'Hell will freeze over before Dan Ragan musters the sand to come for 'em.'

That could be true. Hob was trying to show Ragan how vulnerable he was, trying to ranch in the same neighborhood with a deadly enemy. Seen in that light, the impounding wasn't quite such a case of malicious mischief. Yet Duff knew he was also trying to get himself out of a corner. Put to it, he wasn't sure that *he* could muster the sand to break with Hob as he had threatened.

He said grudgingly, 'All right. But it's your caper. Don't rope me in on it.'

It was three more days, and the impounded horses had made inroads on the supply of emergency hay he and Hob had cut, before anything further came of it. They were eating supper, and Duff was about to suggest that it was running them out of the hay they were mighty apt to need for Hob to make his point.

Neither of them knew Lois was in miles of them when suddenly she appeared at their door.

She shoved open the door without a knock and stepped over the threshold and stopped again. Her eyes were on fire. Glancing out the window, Duff saw two men still sitting their horses out there. They were both tough looking customers, and their six-guns were plainly in evidence.

'Take a real good look,' Lois said. 'They're every bit as tough as you two are.'

Duff saw that Hob had been inspecting the yard, himself. A puzzled, challenged amusement showed in his eyes. He switched his glance to Lois. Her head reared back. If ever there was contempt in a pair of eyes, it was in hers.

'They look real proddy,' Hob agreed. 'When did you start running with company like that?'

'Since you stole those horses,' Lois returned.

'Stole? Why, they're strays.'

'Then why have you got them corralled?'

'They're impounded. Till your daddy pays the feed bill they run up.'

'Strays, my foot!' Lois blazed. 'You're not only land grabbers! You're a pair of plain horse thieves! Those horses were driven here from the other hollow, and don't try to tell me different!'

Duff cut a glance to Hob. He saw from Hob's startled eyes that she was right. Hob had deceived him so he could get away with his stunt. He had gone into the other fork deliberately to get hold of the horses. Duff had to bite his tongue to keep from blowing up, then and there.

If Lois wanted to call it horse stealing and make something of it, she had grounds.

He said mildly, 'What makes you think they were driven onto this side, Lois?'

The hot eyes she had used on Hob turned to ice on him. 'Miss Ragan, to you,' she spat. 'I missed them the day before yesterday. I found the sign and followed it till I knew what had happened. I'm plain sick and tired of it. So I went to town and hired help. They're working for us as long as you two squat in this hollow. Maybe that will make you think twice from here on.'

'*You* hired them gunslingers?' Hob asked. 'What's the matter with your pappy? Hiding behind your petticoats?'

'He's up the country.' Lois stamped her foot. 'Has been the past week. And I'm here because I want our horses, and I want them right now.'

'Fork over eighteen dollars for the feed bill, and you can have 'em,' Hob said.

'Hah.' Lois looked out the door and called, 'Tate? Roscoe? Let out those horses and start home.'

Hob bristled, but he knew he couldn't stop it without a fight. Tate and Roscoe wore thin

85

grins when they swung their horses and, rode toward the corral. It might also have occurred to Hob, as it had to Duff, that, given the initiative, Lois was a different breed than her father. The horses went past the window at a trot. The men behind them appeared to be good at their new job. Then Lois stepped out and pulled the door shut behind her with a bang.

Only then did Hob let his face go slack.

'You think *she's* going to be easy to run off?' Duff asked.

'She don't own the setup over there,' Hob snapped.

Duff said nothing about the deception and trickery. Lois had punished Hob enough by humbling him considerably. Duff admired her, even though she had blamed the mischief on him as well as Hob. But she didn't know Hob as well as he did. This would only be a challenge, and Hob wouldn't rest until he had humbled her in return.

Neither of them finished the supper she had interrupted. They cleaned up from the meal in silence, Hob defensive and touchy, Duff depressed. Hob was already raking his brains for a way to reestablish himself as a specter that even Lois must fear. Duff couldn't help his own melancholy. Her effect on Hob, like his on her, stemmed from that spoiled, impossible attraction of the long ago. And this was as much at the bottom of things as was the hanging of Burley Loman.

They were undressing to crawl into their bunks, later that night, when Hob said moodily, 'I finally placed them two jiggers. I seen 'em a few times down south. The big one's Tate Peters. The other's Roscoe Higbee. Lois hadn't ought to live with 'em, over there, with Ragan gone.'

Astonished, Duff said, 'What do you care what happens to Lois?'

'She don't deserve what they're capable of,' Hob snapped.

Remembering what had just happened, Duff wasn't so sure that Lois wasn't capable of taking care of herself. He said, 'I wonder how she got hold of a pair like that?'

'You can walk into any saloon in Dalles City and find a handful.' Hob hesitated. Then he said reluctantly, 'Maybe you better tell Mandy to warn Lois. They've got records in Nevada that make polecats smell fragrant.'

Duff studied him thoughtfully. If only there was some way to make Hob and Lois see the better side of each other. She could do more for Hob than a hatful of Rubys. If Hob would only start thinking of becoming a family man, as Duff wished heartily he could himself, he would quit gambling the future because of the past. But that was another dream. Hob would never forgive Lois for deriding his young hurt and anger. She was less apt than ever to humble herself and retract.

CHAPTER EIGHT

Duff began to hope again when, the next morning, Hob showed the same uneasiness about Lois's safety. He didn't express it directly. But he was moody and thoughtful while they ate breakfast. It broke out of him finally.

'The work isn't pushing us very hard,' he commented. 'Why don't we make another little visit to town?'

Duff looked up quickly, but Hob avoided his eyes. Nonetheless, Hob was pushing him to see Mandy as soon as possible and tell her what they knew of Peters and Higbee. Duff thought it was wise, himself, although Lois might see it as an effort to make her get rid of her new gun crew. Yet it might open her eyes to the fact that Hob didn't really hate her as much as they both thought.

That settled it, and Duff agreed. To spare Hob further embarrassment, he pretended not to understand the underlying purpose of the visit. To add to the fiction of its being a holiday, he said, 'Why not ride over to the Deschutes landing? We could leave our horses and take the portage train. I been wanting to try that thing ever since I first seen it.'

Hob grabbed hold of the pretense. 'Yeah. Go down today and back tomorrow. That's a good idea.'

They did some inspection riding together, but by midmorning Hob was bored with it and anxious to start for town. The downbound steamboat and connecting portage train wouldn't be at the Deschutes until mid-afternoon. It was hardly an hour's ride to the landing. But they would have to be on their way before Hob would calm down. So Duff said, 'Why don't we get cracking and take our time seeing the sights?'

Hob glanced at him gratefully. 'Might as well.'

They cleaned up, changed clothes and left. Once on the way, Hob grew as elated as if it were a lark and nothing more. In spite of the heavy thoughts nagging him, Duff began to find the man's restored spirits infectious. Autumn in that country was a reversed spring. The sky was clear and blue, the ground dry, and the temperature still mild and pleasant.

They had to cross the Ragan branch of Dutch Creek but did so without seeing anybody. Even so, Duff noticed the quickened interest with which Hob took a look at Ragan's hollow. Then they climbed out on the crinkled plateau that swept from there to the Columbia. It was all empty country. The bare mountains or towering forests in the distances made a queer contrast to the sweeps of sage, seered bunchgrass and crops of rock.

The incongruities struck Hob, too, for he

said, 'Remember how it was back home, Duff? All flat farmland. The same thing to see no matter what direction you looked in.'

'I remember,' Duff said. He didn't know if Hob meant the great valley of California or the Midwest.

Hob pinpointed it. 'Remember what a big excitement it was to us when we finally left the Missouri and struck onto the prairies? Rolling and dry, but still the same everywhere. At least till we could see the Rockies. After them the desert, rolling to the Cascades. Or the Sierras, depending on if you were going to Oregon or California. That was sure a sight.'

'Sure was,' Duff agreed.

It was the first time he had heard Hob refer to their crossing as anything but disaster. Something had made him look back beyond the tragedy. Duff hoped he was right about what, or who, it was.

They rode at such an easy gait they didn't reach the landing until nearly one o'clock. That left only an hour or so to kill there. At that time of day the little river port was quieter than when they saw it with Pike Pelton. The changing seasons were more in evidence there than on the plateau. The trees on the island and screening the settlement were bare of leaves. The headland and rimrock west of the village and the mountains on the Washington bank wore dull winter colors now. The river was lower on the pilings of the long dock. The

Columbia crested in the spring and hit low water around the turn of the year.

Yet, even with no train and no boat in yet, there was a hustle and bustle to the place. Being on the wagon road, it was a waypoint for passersby and freighters using the Spanish Hollow route to the John Day mines. There were saddle-horses and settlers' wagons racked in front of the general store, drawn out of the seeming emptiness. There were Indians about, also, up from the village at Celilo Falls.

There was no regular livery barn, but the hotel operated a public corral. When they had left their horses for the night, Duff and Hob patronized the hotel dining room, which they had almost to themselves. The meal was frontier fare, but Dalles City and its several good restaurants lay ahead. This centered Duff's thoughts on Mandy, herself. He hadn't been near her since Vince Mounts was killed or drowned or whatever had really happened to him. He had to see her now at Hob's behest. He grew uneasy just thinking about it. Considering her coolness when she had only been worried about Mounts, there was little doubt about how she felt now.

The portage train, on its second trip for the day, reached the Deschutes ahead of the downbound steamer. Duff and Hob were killing time on the bench in front of the hotel when they heard the whistle. In a moment or so the train rounded the rocky point, down the river. Short of there the narrow track ran on a trestle. It changed the sound of the engine and wheels. The diminutive cars looked like toys, but they were sturdy, working transports.

Hob had bought a cigar when they came out through the lobby of the hotel. It thrust up at a jaunty angle as he rose to his feet. His look of boyish excitement made it hard to believe that such dark and bitter thoughts could run underneath. They sauntered toward the dock while the train came to a stop. It would be an hour or more making ready to start back to Dalles City. A few dockhands were emerging from the wharfboat to handle the freight. The train crew dropped down, then a few passengers. The latter had thinned to a handful, now. The gold-bearing mountains were less of an attraction with winter so near.

In what seemed like an idle comment, Hob said, 'There's your yellowhead's pappy. Wonder how he'll like our company, going back.'

Duff shot a keener glance along the wharf. Hob's eyes had been sharper than his, or maybe more searching. It took Duff a moment to spot Frank Fleeson. He was in a knot of men waiting for the door of a freight car to be opened. Fleeson hadn't seen them but he looked slack and discouraged. It seemed his natural countenance. He hadn't wrested much from life to make him look otherwise. Duff, could almost pity him, and he could surely pity Mandy.

When Hob lengthened his stride, Duff snapped, 'No you don't.'

Hob glanced at him, frowning. He looked like a dog itching to tree a cat. Then he grinned and shrugged. They went down the other side of the train to the passenger car and climbed aboard. The car was empty except for them. They took seats where they could watch the dock activity through the window.

It was only a few moments until Duff heard another whistle. This one came from up the river. The view was clear from their window, and presently he saw the boat from Wallula and waypoints. It was already rounding the big island, following the Oregon channel. A minute later he saw that she was the big *Harvest Queen*. She rode low in the water because wheat was coming down, now, from the Walla Walla and Umatilla valleys. She had slacked off to make the landing, and steam gushed from her 'scape pipes. Passengers showed on her foredeck, more of them coming out than were going inland. She made her landing in a sudden hubbub of activity.

'One of these times,' Hob said musingly, 'we ought to ride that thing up to Wallula.

Duff glanced at him, nodding his head. Hob seemed to have forgotten Fleeson. His cigar had gone out, but he still had the stub gripped in his teeth. The wharfboat cut them off from the steamer, now, but a few passengers came on across to the dock. Some hurried toward the hotel and bar before boarding the train. They would complain about the dusty ride down the river to excuse their thirst. Others came on into the passenger car and took seats.

The rest of it was duller, causing Duff to reflect that a good deal of western travel was put in waiting. He grew drowsy until he saw the engine come down the siding on the shore side of the main track. It had used the turntable and would couple onto what had been the rear end of the train. The engine swung onto the main line, backed in and made the connection. The dockside activity had slacked off.

All at once Duff was wholly awake. Apparently, when traffic was light, the train hands were allowed to ride with the passengers. A man came aboard looking red-faced and sweaty, and behind him came Fleeson. They walked to the front of the car and sat down, mopping their foreheads.

Fleeson still hadn't noticed who all was in the car. Hob had been looking out the window and apparently hadn't seen the man. The conductor climbed on, and the train whistled, rang its bell, shuddered and began to move. The conductor came along the aisle between the two long seats facing each other, collecting a dollar from each passenger. Hob swung around to pay his fare, and then he saw Fleeson. The man was looking straight at them. He sat like a carved image, even though he wasn't apt to be molested with so many others on hand.

Looking at Duff, Hob said with a grin, 'Small world.'

It was much too small to suit Fleeson. He was still staring, as though hypnotized. The train picked up speed, and Hob joined Duff in watching the passing scene beyond the windows.

In only a few minutes they were whipping past the Celilo falls. They were a wide, tortured sweep of black rock that split the river into countless channels and chutes of deep and raging water. These fell by sweeps and steps into boiling eddies until in a mile or so the water calmed and became again a river.

Duff found this hardly more picturesque than the Indian village strung along the near edge of the falls. There were no wigwams, for these were river Indians who lived in shacks thrown together of brush, straw and dried hides. There were swarms of naked children. Dogs roamed the village, too, and barked ill-temperedly at the train. He could imagine the stench and the swarms of flies.

Beyond these tawdry, sun-baked structures he could see the buck Indians dipnetting from platforms built dangerously over the eddies. They had ropes tied around their waists in case they lost footing and went in. The autumn run of salmon was on, and they were harvesting all they could of it for food for the winter. Squaws and children were hanging strips of salmon on poles to dry in the sun. Duff wondered how much of the fish the flies left for the Indians.

Below the falls the bare Oregon mountain moved back, separated from the river by a flat of rock, sand and brush. Ten Mile Rapids were a scaled-down repetition of Celilo. Sand dunes began to rear beside the tracks, but there was no drifting that day, and the train chuffed on. Five Mile was another rock-tortured rapids covered by fishing Indians. There the river was said to turn on its side, for the constricted main channel had defied all attempts to measure its depth. A mile or so down was Big Eddy, a gigantic whirlpool that, wild as it was itself, tamed the river to flow reasonably from there to the Cascades. Duff was glad to have seen for himself the whys and wherefores of the portage railroad. Not long later the train pulled into Dalles City. The day was all but gone when it stopped to let off passengers at the Umatilla House before the cars were let down to the dock by the steam winch.

Rooms were no longer scarce and, registered, they found themselves in a good one on the second floor. 'Well, where do we start?' Hob asked. 'Want to go over to the wagon yard and see if Pike's in town?'

'Go on, if you want,' Duff said. 'I might go up and see Mandy before her supper rush starts.'

Hob nodded. That was what he wanted Duff to do, but be still wouldn't admit it. 'Good idea,' he said casually. 'I'll drop in on Pike, if he's there.' He studied for a moment. 'You don't like him, do you?'

'Well—he bothers me.'

'Why?'

'He's hard to get hold of.' Duff didn't care to mention his feeling, from the start, that there were things between Hob and the man he hadn't been let in on. 'Anyhow, I can't get hold of him. It seems to be you and him that hit it off.'

'Yeah, we do,' Hob agreed. 'I don't find him hard to know at all. Supposing we meet back here and have supper in about an hour.'

They separated on the street, with Duff wondering if they would see each other again that evening. Once Mandy had the message, Hob's willynilly interests were apt to keep them separated again. He decided that, if they did meet for supper, he would stick to Hob like a cockleburr, no matter what Hob wanted to do.

Mandy's place turned out to be nearly empty, but only Mandy's helper was there. When Duff asked where Mandy might be found, the woman said indifferently, 'She went down on the boat yesterday. Won't be back till tomorrow.'

'Down to Portland?'

The woman nodded, offering no more.

Frowning, Duff went back to the street. He was strongly disappointed, considering how he had dreaded seeing Mandy with Mounts' death hanging between them now. He wondered if he should hunt up the Ragan town house on the chance of finding Lois there. It wasn't likely that he would. She had been at Dutch Hollow the night before. She had said her father was up country somwhere. Hob's warning about the rough characters she had hired would have to keep a while.

He went back to the hotel and again found himself idling on the porch and waiting for his partner. It was nearly an hour, and the street was dark and lamplighted, when Hob showed. Pelton was with him. They were talking, earnestly when they tramped into sight. Duff scowled, hoping the two didn't figure on spending the evening together. He got up and met them when they came up the porch steps.

Pelton nodded and flashed him a grin. But instead of accompanying them into the lobby, he went over to where some other men were sitting on the porch. That suited Duff fine. They walked through the lobby to find that the dining room was open and busy already. Hob nearly always ate there when he was in town, but the place was a little too elegant for Duff. He felt silly being bowed to a table with Hob and having his chair pulled out for him. Hob took over, ordering a fancy meal and a bottle of wine.

'We'll live like this all the time,' he said. 'When we've made our killing in the mines.'

'We've got it to make, first,' Duff reminded him.

'Pshaw, there's no, question about it.' He looked at Duff inquiringly, hoping he would report voluntarily on his errand. When nothing was forthcoming, he said, 'See your yellow head?'

'She went down to Portland. Won't be back till tomorrow.'

'Then we'll lay over a day.' That seemed to suit Hob just as well. The town spirit had worked on him. 'You see old Frank anywhere?'

Duff shook his head. 'I wasn't looking for him. Why?'

'He must feel kind of lonesome. Mandy gone. Mounts gone. Ragan up the river. Even Lois is out in Dutch Hollow. And us in town.'

Always it was there, a maggot working in Hob's brain. Duff wished they hadn't encountered Fleeson, and he was to blame for it. If he had stopped to think he would have remembered that the man worked on the portage train. And he, himself, had suggested that way of coming to town. He made no comment, not wanting to keep the subject going any longer than he could help.

The wine helped him to forget it and to relax and enjoy the heavy meal. Afterward he even felt like lighting up a cigar when Hob did.

As yet Hob hadn't made any suggestions about the evening to come. But Duff still meant to stick close to him. If anything happened again, he wanted to be sure where Hob was at the time. They paid their bill and, going out through the lobby, Hob said, 'You remember that purser in the game I was in, the last time we come down here?'

'Fellow in a boat cap?' Duff asked.

'That's the man. He told me about a honkytonk on the other side of the river. It got run out of this town and set itself up over there. I was about to go over there with him, then I run into Ruby and changed my mind. How about you and me doing it, tonight?'

Duff said, 'Why not?' with a readiness he didn't feel. The last thing he wanted, personally, was a fight or a frolic in a deadfall. But it would put the river between Hob and Fleeson. He hadn't been able to get Fleeson's fear and Hob's excitement, there at the Deschutes, out of his mind. He didn't think Hob had forgotten it, either.

They had to wait for the ferry to steam back from a trip to the other shore. By the time it nosed in and tied, other men were waiting on the landing. Those on foot were probably going to the place Hob had in mind. Three men on horseback and two in a buckboard would be going on. The road that started on the far bank ran to the Yakima.

Standing in the stiffened wind and pulling

on his cigar, Hob said comfortably, nodding northward, 'Some day we'll take a ride into the country over there.'

'Yeah,' Duff agreed.

He kept getting his hopes up in spite of himself. Hob had mentioned a trip up the river sometime. Now this. Like he expected to be alive and free to get better acquainted with the Columbia country.

CHAPTER NINE

The last time Loman and Doncaster came to town, Vince had drowned in the creek. The memory of that was burned on Frank Fleeson's brain as if by a red hot iron. He groped in the darkness of his woodshed until he located a bottle, then tilted it against his mouth and let it gurgle. He had started to put the bottle back when it came to him that he didn't have to hide it from Mandy, not that night. He took it with him into the dark, silent house.

He used a horny thumbnail to flare a match and light a kitchen lamp. The light brought into evidence a reminder that he hadn't cleaned up after last night's supper and this morning's breakfast. He would have to do it before he left for work the next morning. If Mandy came home to find her kitchen mussed up like this, she would be in a temper.

He wished she hadn't picked that particular time to go down the river. He had tried to talk her out of it, for he hadn't drawn a loose breath since the morning he found Vince in the creek. He hadn't for a minute believed that Vince had tumbled off the footbridge. But he hadn't been able to do anything about it. There still wasn't a thing he could do.

Out of habit, he started to kindle a fire in

the stove. Then he realized that he couldn't eat, even if he did make supper. He pushed a dirty plate and cup out of the way and sat down at the table. He had tried to stop Mandy from going by hinting that he knew he was next on the list. That it wouldn't be long before it happened. She had asked him what he thought *she* could do to stop it. He knew there wasn't anything she could do. He just wanted her somewhere near, especially with Dan up the river. Even Lois was out at the horse ranch. Frank knew Lois despised him. Just the same it would be a comfort to know she was in town.

Ordinarily, and if Vince were still around for company, Frank wouldn't have minded Mandy's trip outside. She nearly always went down after the summer rush slacked off at her place of business. She never stayed long and wouldn't this time. She just rested and saw something different and took in the stores and did other things that women liked. She always brought home new clothes, and this time there would be more than usual. For a long while he had thought she didn't aim to get married. Men swarmed around her like flies around a honey jar, but she had no time for them.

Then Duff Doncaster had shown up and turned her wick up bright. Frank abominated the man, but for a while he had hoped they would team up. He would give up his daughter to save his own life anytime. He knew that about himself. He wasn't like Dan, who could persuade himself that whatever he did was the one and only thing that could have been done. Frank admitted in the secret, cringing areas of his own mind, that they had made not one mistake but two, back there.

He tipped up the bottle again and had another long pull. The whiskey hit his stomach but didn't help cut the grease down there. He had missed Vince and grieved for him. Now he damned him for giving Pelton reason to want him shut up. Vince had known that Pelton had a ready-made killer in Hob Loman. The man who, that afternoon at the Deschutes, had given Frank the chilly feeling of looking at Burley Loman, himself.

He had been scared to death of Burley, back there. Maybe that had induced him to throw the entire blame on him for the fight with Amos Bickle, when he testified at the trial. Particularly about the knife. Bickle had actually pulled it before Burley laid a hand on him. Prompted by the way Burley turned and looked at him, after the rock hit the ox in the eye. Burley might have laid his tongue on him and let it go, except for that knife. He had disarmed Bickle with his bare hands and, when Bickle called him an uncivilized son of a bitch, whipped him senseless. And then Burley picked him up and carried him back to the wagon train.

Frank knew that if he had told it like it

happened, the feeling against Burley wouldn't have run so high. He probably would have got off with the banishment Pelton recommended, in place of the hanging Dan ordered. But Frank had known that Dan wanted to fix Burley permanently. The man had made trouble all the way across. He stood for everything that Dan stood against. Dan might even have been scared of him, as Frank and Bickle had been scared. So Frank had cinched it the way he thought Dan wanted it by shading and changing things around a little.

That was their first mistake. The second was just as bad.

Even a nitwit like Vince should have known he could gain nothing by putting Doncaster wise to that letter. That was as senseless as the way Vince tried to use it to squeeze a piece of money out of Pelton. The man who wrote it was lost track of. The letter had been a secret between Dan and Frank at first. Then one night, his tongue loose from whiskey, he had let it spill to Pelton.

Then, in the shock following Vince's death, Frank had told Mandy about it. It had made her furious. It wasn't because Vince had tried blackmail but because Dan had decided the best thing to do with the letter was to burn and forget it. Frank had had a hard time talking her out of taking it to the law even now, with nothing tangible to prove a bit of it. But she had finally cooled off and seen that he was right.

Dan was even more set than Frank against giving the sheriff the whole story. And bringing charges against Hob Loman, even if they couldn't ring in Pelton, and getting the protection of the law for themselves. But Dan's reasons were different than Frank's. He would rather risk getting them all murdered than admit he'd been wrong about anything in his entire life.

Frank took another drink, then sat nursing his anger at Vince for bringing the whole thing to a head. In spite of their being on different sides at Burley's trial, Pelton hadn't had it in for them at the start. He had even had his eye on Mandy and would have courted her if she had encouraged it. Except for Vince's lunatic play, he wouldn't have latched onto Hob when he run into him in San Francisco. And none of this would have come about.

Vince would have been a lot smarter if— Frank hesitated. He hardly dared to think of it, then wondered why he hadn't thought of it sooner. He had to see Pelton himself, and at once. He had to tell him what Vince should have. That the letter Vince had tried to use to scare money out of him hadn't existed even at that time. Dan had got one, sure enough, but had put no stock in it and had burned it. Pelton wouldn't be scared of any story somebody might tell if he knew there was no supporting evidence. Instead of egging Hob on, he might use his influence to hold him back. And he must have considerable influence. Hob would think a lot of the man who had tried to defend his father's life.

Frank had another but smaller drink. His hope was still feeble, but it was hope. He would check it with Dan, if Dan were in town, to make sure he wasn't doing a desperately foolish thing like Vince had done. But it seemed so simple. Just cool Pelton down, and their chances of living were better.

He started to blow out the lamp, then decided he would rather have light in the house when he came back. That might be late, because he didn't like it here when he was all by himself. He left the house and crossed the footbridge with the tightening of the throat that had bothered him every time he used it lately. He still felt boogery when he came to the more built-up part of the street, where there were lighted windows here and there.

He didn't ease off much when he came to the main street. There were still lots of people in sight, and most of the businesses were still there. Not a person there could be called his friend, yet he felt a little better because of them and their numbers.

He slowed going by Mandy's place and saw through the window that there was still trade. That was important to Frank, although he had worked steadily now for quite a while holding his drinking down to where he could still report at the dock every morning to ride the train. This had been less his choice than Mandy's, for she had laid down the law about it. Even so, her business was a comfort to him. Sooner or later he would go on one that would last a week. Then he would once more be out of a job.

If he lived. He remembered his errand with the grease again coating the inside of his stomach. Pelton, when he was around, was one of the regulars at Vic Trevitt's saloon. He had living quarters behind his office at the wagon yard. Frank turned into the saloon, entering hesitantly because his own haunts were the cheaper ones. Nobody paid any attention to him while he satisfied himself that Pelton wasn't there.

He went on to the wagon yard to find the whole place dark. He hadn't taken into consideration that Pelton might be out of town. The chance set his heart leaping in his chest. But there were more saloons to try. And the parlor houses. And sometimes Pelton spent an evening at the dance hall swinging the jezebels.

The man wasn't to be found in any of those places.

Frank needed a drink, for he had devoted himself entirely to his fruitless search. So he went over to Second and into one of his own haunts. There he ran into the closest thing he had to a friend, Alf Madden, the other helper on the cars. Sometimes they weren't on speaking terms, again they got along pretty well, and there had been no recent friction between them.

Madden stood off to himself at the bar, and it was evident that he had been putting away the tanglefoot. He had a wife and children, but every so often he cut loose his wolf. Frank moved in beside him and said with false cheer, 'You ought to leave a little of that stuff for the rest of us, Alf.'

Madden looked at him with unfocused eyes. Recognition came slowly, and he didn't seem especially pleased when it did. He grunted. 'Nobody needs to worry about you getting your share, Frank. What happened to your private stock? Mandy pour it out, again?'

'She's still down in Portland. I told you that today.'

'So you did. Well, drink up. Time's running out on you.'

Frank winced, but Madden hadn't meant it the way it hit him.

Madden was no more talkative than he was on the job, but he was company. After a couple of drinks, Frank's spirits picked up. Mandy would be home the next day. There was just the rest of this night, and then there would be somebody around he could rely on. Maybe not caring a hell of a lot, but somebody loyal to him. Maybe he could make a night of it with Madden.

Even that wasn't to be. After a couple more drinks Madden wove off without a word of farewell. Frank envied him for having a woman to go home to. Not just female company, but a woman to share his bed. He'd had two, losing both the way everything slipped out of his hands. He thought of Lydie, Vince's mother, for the first time in many years.

She had been a widow with a half-grown boy none too bright. But she had also had a little piece of money from her first man. Frank hadn't drunk much, then. While he didn't do too well on the ground he was scratching, back there, they got along after they got married. But she died on him inside of a year.

He had kept Vince, although he could have looked up Lydie's relatives and turned the boy over to them. Or put him in an orphanage. He hadn't fathered him, owed him nothing. Yet he was company. He had taken to Frank from the start. He made a fair hand with the work, and once he was bigger he made a good one. He had kept that feeling to the day he died. Since few had cared for him that much, Frank had got to thinking of him as his own son.

Frank pushed a fingertip along under his eyes, no longer damning Vince but missing him. He signaled the bartender for another.

The second woman had been Helen, and it still mystified Frank why she had married the likes of him. She was the sister of Dan's wife,

110

Lottie, and they were as pretty as any women in the community. Dan had been a combination farmer and preacher, like served in so many of those rural districts. Hard-nosed, wrathful, everything cut and dried. With no backup to him once he had been given the light that guided him.

Helen had lived with Dan and Lottie, slowly turning into an old maid. She was so man-shy she couldn't get her eyes off the ground when one was near. Frank has sensed a loneliness in her even greater than his own, which had drawn him. To his surprise, Dan encouraged him in this. To his astonishment, Helen finally agreed to marry him, causing him to wonder secretly if Dan had crowded her into it.

They had it done by Dan in Dan's parlor, nobody invited in. Mandy had been born to them the next year. The following year Helen came down with typhoid. Lottie nursed her, caught it, and they died within a week of each other. He was left with Vince and Mandy. And, once more surprising him, with Dan, who had Lois to bring up by himself.

While Dan had never considered him of much account, he continued to treat him as kin. Maybe Dan had his own loneliness. He served his fellowmen but didn't befriend them or let them befriend him. Such affection as he possessed was spent on Lois, with a highly diluted form of it left for Frank and Vince. Dan hadn't been interested in marrying again, so Frank didn't look around anymore, himself. They went on scratching out livings, Dan occupying his Sunday pulpit to preach hellfire and brimstone. The two girls got to be like sisters, both of them pretty and dainty as you please.

Then Dan got the bug to go West. Everyone was getting it, those days, hearing so much about how there were no poor out there. If Dan wanted to go, so did Frank. He'd got to depending on Dan because Dan was smarter than he was, tougher than he was. Where Frank knew he was short on backbone, Dan had one stiff as a stove poker.

So they had sold out, packed up and come.

Frank had another drink in this stinking saloon so far from there. Almost homesick from thinking about the places and people put behind. His lot had been hard, there, but he had been safe from violent men who killed as easy as they drew breath. He wanted to go back. Mandy wouldn't listen to such an idea, herself, but she wouldn't much care if he went. She might even let him have the money to travel on.

But, Frank remembered, he wouldn't see her until after this night was over. There was quite a lot of it left. He saw by the clock ticking away above the back bar that it was still short of midnight. He left the saloon, very unsteady on his feet. He went directly up Second, heading toward home but not wanting to go there. He wished he had a key to Mandy's place so he could sleep there in the back room. Yet he tramped mechanically onward, having no choice.

He was hardly halfway home, walking along a street whose houses had grown dark, when the cat cut out of a bushy yard and streaked across the road ahead of him. Even though he knew what it was, Frank hauled up with his heart threatening to stop. It wasn't even a black cat, and when he saw it dart into the darkness again, he grew angry with himself. A man his age, spooked as a woman or an imaginative child. He got a grip on himself and went on toward home, walking faster.

Even so, it was hard to approach the bridge over the creek. When he saw it ahead of him, he slowed his steps in spite of himself. His darting eyes tried to probe the shadows on either side. He could see nothing unfamiliar there. On the other hand, he couldn't see for sure that everything looked familiar there.

He went on, forcing his legs to take steps. Nothing bad reached out for him when he stepped onto the bridge and put a hand on the railing, for support. He crossed with shuttling eyes on the shadowy bank on the far side. He stepped off and went on toward the house, and nothing had happened at all. The lamp he had left burning in the house was the cheeriest sight be had ever seen.

He heaved a sigh of relief but had to stop

and look back to make sure. He went on into the house, passing quickly through the dark sitting room into the lighted kitchen. Everything was as he had left it, including the bottle of whiskey on the table. He picked up the bottle gratefully and took a long pull. He sat down in the chair, in no hurry to go to bed. Maybe he wouldn't. He wouldn't get much sleep, if he did.

His mind was made up. He would tell Mandy, the first thing, that he was going back home. She would know he was running away, but he couldn't help that. She had never had much of an opinion of him, anyway. She had something in her makeup that hadn't been in her mother and himself. Another drink, and he began to see what he contemplated, not as shameful, but as a generous action on his part. Free of Vince and him both, Mandy could do as she liked. He would tell her in a way to make it look like he was only doing what was best for her. Sacrificing himself.

Dan would give her what looking out for she needed until she took a husband. Doncaster, if her heart was set on him. She wasn't an unnatural girl. She wanted a man and children, the same as any woman. Freed of ties, she would have no trouble at all. He was a little proud of himself for standing aside.

He had lifted the bottle again when he heard what sounded like the scrape of a foot on the floor. He sat frozen, the bottle at his lips untasted. He heard nothing and decided that what he had already heard was the scraping of a limb somewhere. When it was windy, several brushed against the house. He didn't remember, though, that it had been windy.

He put down the bottle to get up and look when the thing dropped in front of his eyes. It cinched tight around his throat. When he clawed at it, it jerked hard, and pain shot up through his head and down his back.

His clawing hands recognized the feel of hemp, found the slipknot. Like a hangman's knot. Lights flashed and black spots swirled before his terrified eyes. He thought he was screaming but knew he was only trying to affix sound to the thought in his mind. The protest that they had truly believed they were doing the right thing back there. Then the rope yanked him again. Something snapped. He didn't know it when he crashed to the floor.

CHAPTER TEN

Duff awakened with a groan, punished by his lack of training in Hob's brand of fun. His head expanded and contracted like a beating heart. Each thump made him squeeze his eyes instead of opening them to see whose bed he was in and if it were day or night. He had pleased and challenged Hob by going with him to the honkytonk across the river. It had inspired Hob not only to test his capacity for booze but to sic a particularly persistent girl on him. One that wouldn't take no for an answer.

Duff reached out hesitantly. There was no one there in bed with him, not even Hob. Presently Duff recalled leaving the deadfall and starting back across the river. By then he was seeing two of everything, and his legs had declared their independence of each other. He remembered crossing back on the ferry with Hob, and that was all.

He remembered why he had been keeping track of Hob and opened his hot, grainy eyes. It was broad daylight. The other half of the bed had been slept in, but Hob had beat him up, for once. Duff sat up and waited for the rift that opened in his head to close again. Then he hauled himself out of bed, pulled his watch from its pocket and saw that the forenoon was half gone.

He poured water out of the pitcher and drank it thirstily. He sloshed some of the cold water over his hot face and aching head. They were staying over a day, he recalled, so he could talk to Mandy. He was glad her boat wouldn't be in until the end of the afternoon. He looked at his clothes, which showed no damage. He decided to let a barber shave him. He'd cut his throat if he tried it himself. He dressed and went down to the lobby.

The prospect of reclining again was more attractive than the thought of breakfast. He went into the first barbershop he found and got his shave and added a haircut. When he came out again, he at least looked human. He decided he could handle some coffee and walked up the street toward Mandy's. Even though she was away, he could give her his business.

The blinds of the place were still drawn. A sign on the door said CLOSED.

Duff blinked his eyes. A man in an apron and leather cuffs stood in the doorway of the butcher shop next door. He seemed to be idling, so Duff walked over to him.

He nodded toward Mandy's place and said, 'You know why they're still locked up?'

'Mandy's girl didn't think it was fitting to keep open,' the butcher said. 'So she locked up and went home.'

'Fitting? What do you mean?'

'You know the family?'

Duff nodded.

'Well, old Frank hung himself, last night.'

Duff stared at him, dumbfounded. 'Hung himself?'

'That's the way Alf Madden found him, this morning. Dangling from a rafter in his woodshed.'

Duff shook his head in disbelief. His first benumbed thought was of Mandy. She would be coming home in a few hours to that. Her affection for her father could not have been deep. It would be a nasty shock, just the same. His anger flared against Fleeson, who had taken a miserable, weakling way out of his troubles. It spread to include Hob for creating the fear that had pushed the man over the brink.

The butcher was eager to divulge what information he had about it. Madden was the other train hand, he said. Fleeson hadn't shown up for work, and Madden knew he had drunk heavily the night before. He also knew that, if Fleeson missed work because of drunkenness again, he would be fired. So he had rushed over to Fleeson's to check on him.

Duff nodded and walked away. So now Hob was down to one enemy. One of those gone had been removed by an act of God, the other by his own hand.

Duff hauled up on the street, staring blankly at the busy scene ahead. He didn't really know

118

that Hob had turned in when they got back to the hotel from the honkytonk. Hob had come to bed eventually, but he alone knew when. Maybe it hadn't been a game with Hob, seeing who could drink the other under the table over there. Maybe there had been more than amusement behind his trying to team his partner up with a girl.

He found Hob sitting on the Umatilla House porch, alone and looking somber. Instead of rising, he motioned Duff to come over where he was.

'It looks like you heard.' Hob shook his head. 'Jesus. I never dreamed he'd do a thing like that.'

'He done it,' Duff snapped. 'How did you hear about it?'

'I run into the livery man. He'd just sent a wagon to take Fleeson to the funeral parlor.'

Duff winced. That was where Mounts had been taken, only a short time before. Hob had been lightly dismissing of that death, but now he was scared. The rope Fleeson had used. The gallows Hob had carved and sent through Ragan's window. The bold invasion of Dutch Hollow with the cattle. It was inconceivable that Ragan wouldn't go to the sheriff now. The sheriff was apt to see the two deaths as much more than coincidence.

Hob said softly, 'Even you think I did it.'

'Did you?'

'I didn't.'

119

'Did you hit the hay when I did, last night?'

Hob nodded his head.

'Then don't worry about it.' After a moment, Hob said, 'Thanks.'

Duff knew he had made himself an accomplice in everything if, later, he learned that Hob had deceived and used him. He was far from convinced that this wasn't the case. There had been Hob's deception in connection with the Ragan horses he had tried to impound. His pleasure in driving fear into the marrow of his enemies. His secretiveness.

Duff said impatiently, 'Let's take the afternoon train. There's no use trying to talk to Mandy now.'

'I guess not,' Hob agreed.

He was more subdued than Duff had ever seen him. If he had only been playing cat and mouse, maybe he would stop it. He clung to Duff for the rest of the morning. When noon came, they ate at the hotel. In early afternoon they rode the train to the upper landing. They paid the feed bill on the horses and saddled them. And, at the stage road they had to cross, they ran squarely into Dan Ragan.

He came from up river and wouldn't know yet about Fleeson. He recognized them even as they did him. His countenance darkened. He seemed about to go on, ignoring them. Then he pulled his horse over to the edge of the road where they waited for him to pass on before they crossed. His eyes were icy, his face like rock.

He looked directly at Hob and said coldly, 'My daughter sent me word that you've been meddling with my horses.'

'She tell you,' Hob returned, his meekness gone, 'about the gunhawks she's hired?'

'She told me. Under the circumstances, it meets with my approval. You've got a bone in your throat, and you come here to make trouble. I'm warning you. I've took all I'm going to take of it. That clear?'

Hob knew what Ragan was most apt to do after the discovery he would make in Dalles City. But he said hotly, 'You just think it's all you're going to take! There's nothing I could do short of hanging you that would collect for what you did to me!'

Ragan's eyes widened. Duff's body went cold. Hanging? Hob hadn't realized how this sounded after what had happened the night before.

Ragan said stolidly, 'I warned you, Loman.'

'And I warned you.'

Ragan rode on.

After a long moment, Duff looked at Hob with angry eyes. 'You guaranteed that you'll be answering questions. Maybe before night.'

'I just couldn't take that haughty son of a bitch laying down the law to me.'

'You threatened to hang him. Right on top of Fleeson hanging himself.'

'I didn't threaten any such thing. I told him

121

it would take that to pay for what he done to Burley.'

'And implied that you aim to make him pay for it.'

'I do. And I will.'

Nothing had changed. Nothing would except to worsen matters, and Duff knew he, himself, was caught in it irretrievably.

They rode on toward Dutch Hollow. Again they crossed Ragan's half without seeing anybody. That time, Hob showed no interest in it. They rode over the separating plateau, and it gave Duff a slight lift to see the fork where they had established themselves. Hob didn't seem any more interested in it than in the other hollow. It wasn't the actual possession of all of Dutch Hollow that he wanted. It was coming into possession of it that attracted him. They had eaten supper that evening when Hob said, 'I know what makes you so glum. By now, Mandy's home.'

Duff shot him a look of quick anger. That wasn't all that depressed him, but it had started to add to his gloominess as the day reached its end.

'Too bad,' Hob said, when he drew no answer. 'But how can she blame you if she can't blame me for it?'

'She'll blame you,' Duff exploded. 'Even if she believes Fleeson took his own life, she'll still blame you. And I blame you. None of this has done Burley Loman a speck of good. It won't bring him back.'

Hob said softly, 'You hanker to marry the yellowhead?'

'It makes no difference now.'

'You don't have to stick with me a minute longer than you want.'

'I know that. You remember it, too.'

They stared at each other like enemies, they who had been so close since they were fuzzy-cheeked boys.

CHAPTER ELEVEN

The sheriff was Brig Langford, a veteran of the frontier who policed a country larger than many eastern states. Duff had seen him on the town streets and so knew at once that the worst had happened when he rode in to the camp the next morning. Hob stared out the window, as Duff did, his face grown dark and worried.

Beyond the mounted figure, the sky was filled with an ominous sootiness. This reminded that Indian Summer was gone, that the high desert would soon be under winter's full assault. Langford wore a sheepskin against the cold. He hadn't troubled to pin his star on the outside and didn't need it. The look of him carried authority enough.

'Ragan lost no time,' Hob muttered.

'Blame him?'

'He threatened me as much as I threatened him.'

'That's not what Langford's here about.'

They had eaten their breakfast in sullen, silence. Silent again, they watched Langford swing down and drop reins. He knew they hadn't yet left the dugout and might have noticed them looking out the window. He didn't conduct himself like he expected trouble, but his six-gun rode where it would be easy to fist.

His chin, setting aggressively, Hob rose, went over and opened the door. Duff followed him, trying to conceal his worry. Langford looked at them mildly, but there was no doubt of what was on his mind.

He said, 'Morning, boys.'

'Howdy, sheriff.' Hob had got hold of himself. His voice was as easy as if he were greeting any acquaintance arrived at his door. 'Come in. You're just in time for breakfast.'

'Ate before I left town. You're Loman, ain't you?' Hob nodded. Langford glanced at Duff. 'And you're Doncaster.'

'That's right.'

'I need a little information from you boys.'

'Why, sure,' Hob said agreeably. 'Come in and have some coffee, anyhow.'

'That would be welcome. It's turned damned chilly.'

Duff thought he was being a little too relaxed and casual. But Langford's cool eyes contradicted that. They were sizing things up. He came in, went to the stove and started warming his hands in the heat. He declined Hob's suggestion that he take off his heavy coat and even kept on his hat.

Hob poured him a cup of coffee. Langford took it and sipped. 'That's cow camp coffee. The kind I like. I heard you boys were in town yesterday.'

'That's right,' Hob agreed.

'Heard you knew Frank Fleeson.'

'Sort of,' Hob said. 'We come west in the same wagon train.'

'So I heard. And that there's been bad blood between you and that bunch ever since.'

'Who told you about that?' Hob asked easily. 'Dan Ragan?'

The sheriff shook his head 'Mandy. Fleeson's girl.'

Duff could hardly keep from blinking his eyes. Even Hob was surprised. And a little relieved, for neither of them thought that Ragan would have told her about the brush at the Deschutes and left it to her to go to the sheriff. If they were right, Langford didn't know about what Ragan must have taken for a threat against his life.

'No reason why you shouldn't know,' Hob said. 'But I don't see why she brought that up. It happened a long time ago.'

'Mandy don't think her dad hung himself.'

'Who does she think hung him?'

'She left it to me to find out. It seems queer a man of his cut would use a rope on himself. It's a mean way to die.'

'Don't I know it?' Hob's voice turned cold.

'You ever threaten him?'

'Then. I was a button and mighty upset. They gave my dad a mighty raw deal. Talk to Pike Pelton. He was there. He'll tell you a different story than Ragan tells.'

'I ain't talked to Ragan.' Duff hoped he

126

concealed his relief as well as Hob did. 'Not about this. And I won't need to take up more of your time if you can tell me what you did after midnight, the night before last?'

'That's easy. I was in the hay asleep. Why?'

'A man called Madden seen Fleeson in a saloon just before midnight. He was alive then. And dead at six o'clock, when Madden went to his house to see why he hadn't come to work.'

Every gut in Duff's belly churned. Between midnight and morning. Hob's glance shot to him and slid away. Hob wasn't sure of him now, after their row. Duff wasn't sure, either, what he would say. Telling the truth about his own drunken sleep, during that period, would make it worse for Hob. But Duff was thinking mainly of Mandy. Lying to protect the man who might well have murdered her father would cut the last frayed strand binding them.

He seemed to hear a stranger talking, although it was his own voice. 'If that's what you've been getting at, Langford, forget it. Unless Mandy's got you suspicious of me, too.'

Langford shook his head. 'She took pains to exclude you, Doncaster.'

That only made it harder. 'Well, then. Hob and me had supper at the Umatilla House. You can check that. Then we went across the river to that deadfall over there. You can check on that, too. Somewhere about midnight, we come back to the hotel and turned in. He wasn't out of my sight once during all that time.'

'Up to midnight,' the sheriff said.

It had to come now, the truth or the lie. 'All night. He couldn't have got to the door, even, under his own steam. We had some drinks in the room, too, and Hob went out like a light. We'd swilled a lot of rotgut in that honkytonk, and it scared me. I was up half a dozen times to see if he was all right'

Hob's lips creased in a slight smile.

Langford rubbed his jaw. He looked relieved. Fleeson had been a no-account, one of the town's habitual drunkards. After a moment, be said, 'I reckon that lays the dust.'

He was soon on his way, and Duff found it impossible to look at Hob.

Hob said softly, 'Thanks. He'd never have believed that, if it had come from me.'

'He damned near didn't, coming from me. He wouldn't have believed it for a minute if Mandy hadn't put in a good word for me.'

'Yeah. It looks like she's gone on you, too.'

Duff wanted to hit him. Hob seemed to have no conception of what the moments just passed had cost.

Duff spent the day in the saddle, riding alone, starting out on the plateau between the two forks of Dutch Creek. Every steer he found near Ragan's edge he drove closer to home, now that Hob had made straying an explosive issue. He didn't find much besides that to do, but he killed time. Things weren't

128

the same, anymore. He preferred his own company to Hob's.

He was ready to circle south and turn back toward camp to noon when he found the dead steers. There were three of them, all shot through the head They were cold and stiff and must have been killed while he and Hob were in town. They were on Ragan's side, if the line were drawn halfway between the two hollows, dividing the plateau equally.

Duff sat there a long while, his stomach full of rocks. He wished he could keep this from Hob but knew it was out of the question. Hob poked around at random, the same as he did, with them agreeing at breakfast which part of the range each would cover that day. Except for the bones, these carcasses would carrion off before long. But skulls with bullet holes would tell the whole story. Hob's finding them sooner would be no worse than his finding them later, as he surely would.

Yet he didn't tell Hob about it at noon. Nor could he bring himself to it that evening. For the next three days he got away with picking the north side for himself to ride. On the following morning, Hob broke it up.

'Whatcha got over there?' he asked. 'A gold mine? Or is it you don't trust me that close to the north fork?'

'All right.' Duff shrugged. 'There's dead steers at the head of the hollow. Three. Shot. On Ragan's side of the plateau. I found 'em

129

the forenoon after we come back from town.'

Hob gaped. 'And never said a word about it.'

'Because there's nothing to do about it. You called the tune on strays. Now we've got to dance to it.'

Hob shook his head disbelievingly. 'You expect *me* to just swallow it?'

'I expect you to get this through your head. Ragan's not going to let himself be run out of Dutch Hollow.'

Hob said nothing, but there was a queer light in his eyes.

Duff rode the north range again, and Hob didn't protest. Within an hour, Duff was glad he had been stubborn. Well on the south side of the line, he found half a dozen Ragan horses. The minute he sighted them, something bothered him. Horses were more rangy than cattle. But, like cattle, they were inclined to stay in familiar surroundings. There was no water near where he found them to lure them. The grass was no better than where they had come from. So he scouted for sign, riding between the animals and Ragan's hollow, and he found it. The horses had been driven deliberately, as the first bunch had been.

Hob again? There would be no point in it. Besides, there hadn't been enough time since he heard about the shot steers.

Duff wished he had looked for evidence of similar mischief after he found the dead steers.

This at hand suggested that somebody besides Hob was trying hard to pick a real hot fight. It couldn't be Lois, but it could be one of her tough hombres. Trying to stir up both sides of the quarrel, out of pure cussedness, or maybe some secret purpose of their own. Duff knew he had to talk to Lois and hoped she was still at the horse ranch.

He drove the little bunch ahead of him, heading directly north into what now was hostile territory. He was still driving the supposed-to-be-strays when he came down into the hollow near Ragan's headquarters site. He knew before he reached the house that there was nobody there. His hail brought nobody forth, and when he reached the barnyard there was still nobody in sight. He let his little drive drift to a stop at the watering trough.

He was about to leave the bottom, on his way home, when he saw a rider off to his left. He reined in, discerning that whoever it was was heading toward him at a rush. He waited, watching with grim eyes, growing aware that the rider was small. In a moment he knew it was Lois. She held a rifle, which she had pulled out of its boot. Anger darkened her face as she closed the gap.

'You,' she said, relaxing slightly. Apparently she had taken him for Hob. They were both big men, and he had the collar of his sheepskin turned up. 'What are you doing over here?'

131

'I was at the house, as you saw,' Duff said calmly. 'I left you a present.'

'Present?'

'Some strays of yours. Sound and healthy. I dropped them at your water trough.' He nodded at the rifle she still held at the ready. 'You've come a far piece in this country. You stick a horse like it was glued to you. I reckon you can handle that gun just as good.' He nodded off to the southeast. 'There's three steers of ours over there, all shot through the head.'

He saw in her eyes that she knew nothing about that. 'Are you accusing me of shooting them?' she gasped.

'No, but I think one of your men did. After hazing them onto your side so they'd have a flimsy excuse. I think they spotted the horses I brought back on our side. Hoping Hob would find and kill them.'

'You're out of *your* mind!'

'Maybe. But you oughtn't to have those jiggers around. They're pure poison. Hob knew 'em in Nevada. It will surprise you to hear that Hob worried about you. Not about the trouble they might make us. He wanted me to warn you through Mandy. We were in town waiting for her to get home from Portland. Then I heard about Fleeson and knew it was better for me not to see her.'

Lois looked at him with disbelieving eyes: 'I can imagine Hob Loman worrying about *me*,' she scoffed.

'Then don't try, but it happened.'

'So have a lot of other things happened,' Lois said bitterly. 'Including murder. Don't try to throw dust in my eyes, Duff Doncaster.'

'Does Mandy still think Hob killed her dad?'

Lois looked away. Then she said reluctantly, 'She did till you cleared him. She's got a crazy notion you wouldn't lie about a thing like that. I know you would, when it comes to Hob Loman. You'd do anything for him. And you're a damned fool for it.'

Duff was glad she wasn't watching him.

He rode on, having warned her and having learned all he wanted to know. He had grown sure that more was going on than Lois knew about. But maybe not more than Dan Ragan knew about. She had hired the gunmen on her own hook. But Ragan might have seen more use for them than merely protecting his property. After Fleeson's death, he was next in line and had been openly threatened, as Ragan would see it. So he wouldn't mind seeing Hob killed in a range fight. The dead steers and tempting stray horses, Duff grew convinced, had been bait. They were supposed to have drawn Hob into a trap in which Ragan could remove the danger to himself while keeping his own coat tails clean.

When he met Hob at camp at noon, Duff told him about the horses, what he had done with them, and his talk with Lois. 'I don't think she's onto everything anymore than I am,' he said in conclusion. 'But I know this. You outsmarted yourself. At least you've let Ragan outfox you. Handed him a fine way to get the south fork cleared. And you off his back, in connection with the rest, as a bonus.'

Hob was sobered by it, himself. He knew if he had found the steers or horses, either one, he would have gone smoking into something neatly set up that could have cost him his life.

'You could be right,' he admitted. 'That coyote would let wolves do his killing. The way he got that wagon company to hang Burley, because he was scared to have him in the train.'

'If you could only forget that—'

Hob turned on him with a hostility Duff had never seen there, in relation to himself. 'Sure. Just play like it never happened. Because Dan Ragan's got himself some gunhawks to fight his battle.'

'Well, don't make it easy for him.'

'You can bank on it. I don't aim to do that.'

CHAPTER TWELVE

The nights had long been frosty, and by late November the daytime temperatures hung below freezing, too. There was worse to come, Duff knew. Another month would bring the deep winter, which he dreaded but awaited, also. Its passing would bring spring when he and Hob could hit the trail for the mines. Sometimes he dared to hope that this could come about without more trouble.

He had a feeling that Lois had laid down the law, for there was no more mischief from the horse ranch. As far as he knew, Hob had made none. Hob didn't even talk about it, anymore. Nor did he spin dreams about the big cattle ranch they would build, after they had frightened Ragan out of Dutch Hollow. Hob seemed to have been given pause by the discovery that two could play the game.

At other times, Duff had a feeling that Hob was only waiting. He was more somber than Duff had ever seen him. The weeks went by without his suggesting another lark in town. Nor did Duff have any desire to visit Dalles City again, himself. He had betrayed the faith Mandy had in him. He couldn't face her again.

And then, in early December, everything went berserk again. Hob came walking in, one freezing day, carrying his saddle. Duff had beaten him to camp by nearly an hour. He had the stove throwing out heat, with the noon meal started. It was only by chance that he glanced out the window to see Hob trudging across the flat from the southeast. The sight sobered but didn't alarm him, for the main danger didn't lay off in that direction. The ground was frozen, with slick spots to be watched for. He surmised that Hob's horse had hurt itself. Probably a broken leg, which doomed a mount when it happened miles from anywhere. Hob seemed to be all right himself.

Duff was standing in the doorway when Hob came in. Hob's face was thunderous with anger, announcement enough that this was no routine ranch accident. He only glanced at Duff and dropped the saddle by the doorstep. Duff moved back, let him come inside, and close the door, afraid to ask about it.

'We're out a horse,' Hob said. 'Dan Ragan's out a man. They're both dead at Rock Springs.'

Duff could only look at him and say feebly, 'You mean—you killed one of Ragan's gun hands?'

'You're damned right I killed him. The son of a bitch tried to dry gulch me when I come in to the springs.'

'Which one was it?' Duff managed to ask.

'It wasn't Peters or Higbee. The old coyote hired himself a new wolf. I never seen the cuss before, here or anywhere. But he was Ragan's

136

man. Laying for me there in the rocks. At a place one of us checks every day. So what else can you make of it?

Duff couldn't make it anything but what Hob thought. The only one with a known reason for wanting Hob dead was Ragan. Since Hob hadn't let himself be baited into a trap, one had to be set up where there was no doubt he would move into it. The new man must have been hired especially to do the job and then light out. There would be nothing to tie it to Ragan. The killer could have been a range bum on foot and after Hob's horse and what money he might have on him.

'What happened to the fella's horse?' Duff asked.

'He was afoot.'

Duff nodded. A nice cover-up when the sheriff took a look at the sign. But Duff couldn't believe it had been a tramp, anymore than Hob believed it.

'What are you going to do, Hob?'

'Fetch the sheriff.'

That was some relief. Duff had been sick with fear that Hob would want to settle it personally. Yet Duff still didn't like the feel of it and said uneasily, 'It could snow, the way the sky looked this morning. Maybe, I better take a look, too, while the sign's fresh—and still there.'

'Because Langford would believe you.'

'It helped you once that he does.'

'All right.' Hob shrugged. 'I'll go back with you. He wouldn't come out before morning, anyhow. It'll be dark by the time I hit town.'

Duff took up the food and put it on the table. Hob only drank coffee, lost in bitter thoughts. Duff couldn't eat, either. Then they saddled horses at the corral and rode off toward Rock Springs.

There was nothing to be found there but Hob's lifeless horse and frozen blood behind one of the several huge boulders.

Hob said feebly, 'What do you make of that?'

Duff shook his head, as disturbed as Hob by the discovery. 'It might be he was able to get to his horse.'

'But he was dead,' Hob said insistently. 'He knew when my horse went down that he'd bungled it. I got clear, but he must've figured it had pinned me down, because I just laid there watching. Pretty soon I caught him trying to sneak a look. I got him smack in the forehead. There's no two ways about it. He *had* to be dead.'

'Then there were two of them. One stayed with the horses, while the other sneaked in to get you. That would leave the right kind of tracks.'

'Why didn't the other one try for me, then?' Hob asked bewilderedly. 'I wasn't looking for anybody else. I poked around here a few minutes. Taking a look at him, then getting my saddle.'

'He was off too far to know what happened. Then had to come in when his pardner didn't show back. We better take a damned good look, this time. What we can find is all there'll be to show Brig Langford.'

'No use telling him anything, now,' Hob said angrily.

Even as it was, there wasn't much sign on the frozen earth. Besides the blood behind one of the boulders, there were the tracks made by the shoes of Hob's horse, here and there where they had creased or broken the crust. The lighter man, with leather boot soles, had left hardly any tracks at all. All they could do was ride circle at intervals widening out from the springs. They split for this to save time, and it was Duff who found what they were hunting.

The rest came more easily. There had been two of them. One had waited nearly a quarter of a mile from the springs while the other went in on foot. It would have been a clever, very misleading maneuver if it had come off. The second man had gone in, also on foot, to see why the first hadn't returned. He had carried the body back.

They headed back for camp, riding silently. Only when they were headed in that direction could Duff see the inky blackness gathered over the Cascades, much heavier than it had been at noon. Now it was spreading over the open high country eastward.

'It's really making bag, now,' he said.

Hob glanced at the sky but said nothing. Duff didn't like that kind of closing up, not in Hob.

'Want me to ride to town with you?' he asked.

'I'm not going to town,' Hob shot back. 'They'll bury the son of a bitch. By morning there'll be nothing but my horse to show anything happened at all. That's not enough to hang it on them.'

Duff felt colder than the air about them. Hob had expected to strike a telling blow against his enemies. They had made that impossible legally. So Hob was back to considering other means of doing it.

Hob had pulled back into himself and stayed there while they rode on to camp, put up the horses, and prepared for their supper and the night. Darkness came in accompanied by a strengthening wind. Well as they had chinked the dugout, it began to leak in cold. Now and then the lamp flickered and emitted a puff of smoke.

The next morning snow was falling. Four or five inches of it lay on the window sill.

Duff built a fire, made coffee, sliced bacon, and stirred up batter for flapjacks. Hob lay indifferently in bed, smoking a cigarette, his face thoughtful and withdrawn. Duff knew he had lost interest in everything but what had

140

happened, here and back there on the emigrant trail.

Trying to josh him out of it, Duff said, 'You going to stay there all day?'

Hob grunted something. After a moment, he pushed to a sit on his bunk, the cigarette dangling on his lips. His gaze strayed moodily to the window, and his mouth tightened.

When he still said nothing, Duff tried another tack. He had to get him talking again. 'What did this fella look like?' he asked.

'Nothing special.'

'Everybody looks a little different to anybody else.'

'This jigger was run of the mill,' Hob snapped. 'He was wearing a beat-up old army overcoat. And he had a crop of whiskers. That suit you?'

'It might help to get a line on him in Dalles City,' Duff said.

Hob cut him a look of interest. He hadn't thought of that as a way to trace the ambusher to Ragan. Duff was less interested in that than in getting Hob busy and out of Dutch Hollow until he had calmed down.

'Maybe you got something,' Hob mused. 'But this country's full of whiskers and old army overcoats. Even if somebody seen this jigger, it wouldn't tie him to Ragan.'

'You can't tell.'

At least it offered action, which Hob himself preferred to this baffled inertia. He said with sudden energy, 'No harm in seeing. You want to come along?'

Duff hated the role of watchdog, but he was less inclined than ever to leave Hob to his own devices. The cattle were on the bottom, and they would stay there until the weather cleared.

He said with as much indifference as he could manage, 'Might as well.'

By the time they were ready to leave, he knew he had made a good suggestion. Hob had stopped his yeasty brooding. Movement, however unpromising, had always acted to settle him. Yet he showed none of the usual excitement with which he set out for town. Something quieter but more deadly had entered him.

The ride to town was the slowest in their experience. There were only a few inches of snow on the open ground, although more fell fitfully. The canyons beyond the Deschutes were something else. They lay at higher elevations, were windy, and the snow lay in either thin dustings or in deep drifts. Duff kept an uneasy watch on the sky, wondering if they could make it home again very soon. It might be better, though, for them to be pinned down in town a while, even if they lost a few steers to hungry predators and the weather, itself.

They came to the Columbia at the mouth of Fifteen Mile to see that, at the lower elevation, the snowfall had been lighter. The portage tracks, which ran beside the road from there to Dalles City, showed that the train had made its morning run to the upper landing. The horses could travel faster, after that, and in less than an hour they rounded the rocky point onto the main street of the town. The street had become a familiar sight, and Duff's heart speeded when, not far down, he made out Mandy's sign.

Hob broke a long silence to say, 'I hope Pike's not off up the country. He'd be as apt as anybody to notice our huckleberry, if they were both in town at the same time. Think I'll check on him first. You want to come along?'

Duff didn't answer immediately. Pelton was always the first one Hob thought of when they arrived in town. A desire to talk to him about the ambush might have been part of his reason for coming in. Duff had a feeling Hob hadn't really wanted him to come along. That was enough to decide it. He nodded his head.

Pelton was in his wagonyard office. He had been busy, but he shoved it aside when Hob and Duff walked in. A big grin of welcome spread over his weathered face.

'Well, now. I thought you boys would be snowed in by now, up there in the high country.' They shook hands, and he motioned the visitors to chairs. 'What's new besides the weather?'

'Plenty,' Hob said.

Pelton pushed a cigar box to the edge of the

143

desk. Hob helped himself, but Duff declined. He would never get over feeling uneasy around this man and disinclined to take favors off of him. Pelton struck a match to help Hob light up.

'So?' he said, and waited.

'I killed a man yesterday,' Hob said. 'After he come within an inch of killing me.'

Pelton stiffened. 'The hell you say. How come?'

Hob gave him a full account of it, including the meager description he had of the ambusher. 'You get around a lot,' he concluded. 'Struck me you might have seen him somewhere.'

'Could be I have,' Pelton said thoughtfully. 'Big nose and mean eyes.'

'That's the man.' Hob looked excited. 'His nose was big. And he sure looked mean.'

'Man like that hung around Umatilla Landing a while. Think I heard his name. Something like glanders, that horse disease. Landers. That was it.'

'Umatilla's a long ways up the river,' Duff said.

Hob frowned at him. 'Dan Ragan's up that way all the time.'

Pelton said with interest, 'You think Dan hired him to do away with you?'

'You're damned right I do.'

'Could be.' Pelton nodded his head. 'He's scared enough. And trying to get you locked up didn't work.'

'That wasn't his move,' Duff cut in again. 'It was Mandy's. How come you know about it?'

'I know it was Mandy's,' Pelton said, looking at him thoughtfully. 'But they're one and the same. Langford come to see me after he'd been out to see you boys. Went into that old business about Burley.'

'I told him to check with you,' Hob said.

Pelton nodded. 'I gave it to him straight. Told him what a raw deal Burley got and why that bunch has plenty of reason to be spooked. Which makes them distort your being here all out of shape. That seemed to satisfy him.'

'Thanks,' Hob said.

'On the other hand, I don't think he'd listen to charges against Ragan. At least, without meat to 'em. The distortion could work both ways. You could try to sic him on them to get even for them trying to get you in hot water.'

'You ought to report it, anyway,' Duff said, looking at Hob. 'Somebody tried to kill you. You don't have to say who you think it was. Even if he didn't do much, it ought to be on record.'

Hob gave him a glance that told him whose advice he wanted. He said irritably, 'For once, will you stop acting like a mother hen? I'm not going gunning for Ragan. He'll come gunning for me, himself, when I kill him.'

Duff felt like he had at the Deschutes when Hob lost his temper and reason and seemed to

145

threaten to hang Ragan. He got to his feet.

'Where you going?' Hob said quickly.

'To tend to my own business.'

Duff walked out.

CHAPTER THIRTEEN

Duff had stepped through the doorway of Mandy's place before he realized that something was wrong there, too. It had begun to draw supper trade and was filled nearly to capacity. But a woman he had never seen before was behind the counter. A man was working at the cookstove. Duff shook his head puzzledly, almost believing that, in his preoccupation, he had blundered into the wrong place. But it was the right place. Just the wrong people.

He went to the end of the counter and stood waiting. He didn't want to eat or take up space at rush hour by having a cup of coffee. The woman noticed and regarded him puzzledly. But she went on with her work. She was middle-aged and sour, and the male cook had a slouchy look to him. They didn't fit in Mandy's place at all.

Presently the woman came over to him and said sourly, 'What's on your mind, mister?'

'I'm looking for Mandy Fleeson. Know where I can find her?'

She shook her head. 'Don't know her, except in a business way. We come up from the Coast and bought this place. Just ain't got around to changing the sign.'

'Bought it?' Duff blinked his eyes.

'Lock, stock and barrel. She did say something about trying Portland or maybe 'Frisco. She lost her pa. I do know that. I reckon it made her want a change of scenery.'

Duff had trouble finding his voice. 'Know if she sold her house yet? he asked.

The woman shook her head. 'Like I said. I don't know anything about her personal business.'

Duff mumbled his thanks and walked back to the street. A find faint, fine snow was sifting down. Mandy gone? Of course she had gone, or she wouldn't have sold her means of livelihood. It left him feeling hollowed out and hating himself for letting her get away from him again. He hadn't any hope, but he could try her house and see if it was dark and vacant. Or if new people lived there, they might know more about her. He found himself walking in that direction even before he decided to go. He remembered the night he had walked her home. How she had stopped him at the near end of the footbridge. How she had felt in his arms when, so unexpectedly, she was there.

He came to the bridge again, and the house beyond showed lamplight.

He crossed it fast, and the little flat, and knocked on the door. And Mandy stood there, surprised and yet not so surprised. Like it was halfway natural for him to appear at her door.

'Mandy!' He was too short of breath to talk. 'I heard you sold out! It sure gave me a turn!'

'Hello, Duff.' Things weren't the same, though. Far from it. There was reserve in her pretty face now. Her wonderful voice had an impersonal tone she had never used on him before. She seemed to debate a moment before she even said, 'Come in.'

At least he knew where she was. Could talk to her. It calmed him some.

He followed her through a cramped hall into a sitting room not much larger. A fire burned in the heater, and the room was neat and attractive. Her work. Even the heater had been blackened recently. She didn't take his hat or invite him to take off his heavy coat. She didn't figure on his being there long. She didn't want him there, at all.

He said heavily, 'I wanted to see you after you lost your dad. But I knew you'd detest me. What you'd think.'

'Then why did you come, tonight?'

'I seen Lois. She told me you don't think Hob was responsible for what happened to your dad. Except maybe for scaring him into it.'

'Wouldn't that be bad enough?'

'Bad, all right. And you feel I share the blame for that.'

'Don't you?' She faltered. 'Oh, Duff. Must you be so blindly loyal to that man? Can't you see he's failed you, straight down the line?'

'Hob? Failed me?'

'He's used your devotion from the day

Pelton found him in San Francisco and told him where we were.'

Duff blinked his eyes. It was true. Hob had failed him again only a while ago at the wagonyard. Dismissing him, turning to Pelton for counsel. Hob had failed him every time he did something, callous to the consequences, disregarding everything but what his hatred of his enemies dictated.

But Duff said stubbornly, 'You're wrong. Hob'd lay down his life for me. Any time.'

'Would he?'

Duff turned to go. But something had crawled out of the sealed-off places in his mind, evoked by her mention of Pelton and his own secret outburst against Hob. Duff thought of the night Mounts had tried to tell him something and had been cut off by the arrival of Pelton. Mounts had looked terrified. Why would he care that Pelton saw them talking together? Why had all of them been so suspicious of Pelton's part in Hob's coming to this country?

Duff's jaw set. He wasn't going to walk out of Mandy's life again without getting to the bottom of that. His sheepskin was roasting him in the warm room. He tossed his hat on a chair and took off the coat. Mandy frowned, angry and wanting him out of her sight

'You might as well set down,' he said. 'I'm staying till you tell me why you and all your people were so upset to hear Pike Pelton was mixed up in us coming here.'

'I—' Mandy broke off and dropped into a chair. He took another. Waited. She didn't say any more.

'You knew something that might have kept me clear of all this,' Duff accused. 'When I asked why hc scared you, you wouldn't tell me. Who were *you* being loyal to?'

She shook her head in distress. 'I can't talk about that'

'If you still can't, it's to Dan Ragan. He's the only one left alive.'

She flushed and dropped her gaze so quickly he knew he was right. She looked up and said feebly. 'It was the same thing, wasn't it? I never saw that before. Except for Pelton, Hob might not have done what he has. At least you might have kept your own self in the clear.'

'Except for scaring everybody, what do you think he's done?'

'My father never had the courage to take his own life. Especially with a rope. I think Hob did it. I think he killed Vince and threw him in the creek dead.'

'But you told Lois—'

'That I believed what you told the sheriff,' Mandy cut in. 'That was my pride. I'd always defended you to her. I couldn't agree with her that you lied to get Hob out of it. But you did. And that makes you as guilty of the murder of my father as Hob is.'

Duff couldn't refute that. Nor could he admit it without giving her the means of getting Hob clapped into jail. He said unhappily, 'You want to think he's guilty. I don't. It's easy to find arguments on either side.'

'There's more argument on my side than you know, Duff. That's where I failed you. But I couldn't tell you without incriminating Uncle Dan of what I accused you of . . . Helping to conceal a crime.'

'Amos Bickle.' Duff's words snapped out. 'He didn't die from that fight.'

Her mouth dropped open. 'Why—how could you know that?'

'Mounts started to tell me. Pelton come along and broke it up. That same night Mounts fell off the footbridge and drowned.'

Mandy sucked in a sharp breath. After a moment she said falteringly, 'I couldn't have told you much at the start. All I knew was that something had happened to make all three men scared to death of Pelton long before Hob came here. But that might have been enough to keep you from letting Hob, with Pelton pushing him, drag you into it like he has.'

It wouldn't have made any difference, Duff reflected. He had never trusted Felton, but that hadn't kept him from getting involved.

'That's all I knew and all Lois knows yet,' Mandy continued. 'When Vince was murdered —and he was—my father broke down and told

152

me about the letter.'

'Letter?'

Mandy nodded her head. 'A letter that made it look like Felton might have killed Bickle, the night after the fight. You remember they were wagon partners. Pelton took care of him, and it was him that passed the word, the next morning, that he was dead. He could have smothered him to make sure he died.'

'But why?' Duff gasped.

'Bickle was bringing quite a lot of money with him. He'd sold a business of some kind. But nobody knew that, except maybe Pelton, until Uncle Dan got the letter. Vince was stupid enough to think he could use it to blackmail Pelton. Pelton thinks Uncle Dan's still got it and could use it to make things hot for him even yet. He doesn't know it was burned up.'

The room was hot, but Duff felt cold as the stormy, outdoor night. 'So he's egged Hob into getting rid of them, one by one.'

Mandy nodded, unable to continue, although he waited silently. He was as sick as she was. Hob would never believe he had been betrayed by the man who had been his hero since he was half grown. If Hob had been betrayed. Duff didn't know why Mandy was so sure. Then she began to talk again, telling him as much as she had learned from her father.

Two or three years after the crossing, a relative of Bickle's wrote Dan Ragan in inquiry, having traced and learned that he had died on the trail and that Ragan had been captain of the train. The relative wanted to know what became of the money, some ten thousand in gold, Bickle received from the sale of a business he had inherited and sold to move out to the West. Pelton had taken possession of Bickle's wagon and outfit, it being of little value and there being no heirs around.

The letter had come the closest anything ever had to upsetting the self-certainty of Dan Ragan. Pelton had been stony broke on the crossing, hardly more than a bum. Yet discreet inquiry disclosed that he had arrived in Dalles City to set himself up promptly as an army supply contractor. He had paid for the costly equipment in gold. He was at least a thief. So he could easily have despatched Bickle, the night after the fight, in the privacy of their wagon. In possession of the money, he could have made Burley Loman the goat, defending him only to make himself look good to the rest of the emigrant company.

This might have been checked and proved, for it was still a fairly recent thing, had Ragan been willing to go to the authorities. But to do so would be to expose his own part in a gross miscarriage of justice. It was too much for a man of his set mind. He persuaded himself that the letter was meaningless. If Bickle had had such money, something had happened to

154

it before he started West. Ragan didn't answer the letter, letting the eastern relative think it had never caught up. He had burned it and settled back into his conviction that justice had been done in his primitive court on the trail.

'He knows better now,' Mandy said, with a shake of the head. 'But he's helpless. He helped bury Pike Pelton's crime.'

Ragan's first mistake, she continued, had been in letting Fleeson know about the letter. He should have realized the kind of situation it would create for him. He had done so because Fleeson had known Bickle better than Ragan had and might have learned something of the presence of money in Bickle's wagon. It turned out that Fleeson had known nothing.

Ragan had sworn him to secrecy, but Fleeson had already let it slip to Mounts. When Mounts' blackmail backfired, he ran to Fleeson in fear, and Fleeson ran to Ragan. Even with no letter in Ragan's possession any longer, they did know the truth about Pelton, and that put all three in danger. They had lived in fear of Pelton ever since. Conversely, Felton had lived in fear of being exposed. The statute of limitation might protect him from a charge of theft, but not from a murder charge.

'Brig Langford said it was you that come to him,' Duff said, finally. 'How come you set the law on Hob, if you think he's been Pelton's tool? Why not Pelton, too?'

Mandy flushed and looked down at the

floor. 'Hob's guilty, even if he has been egged on. I thought if he was brought to time, you'd be out of it before he took you down with him. I didn't foresee you'd help him clear himself.'

'You said nothing to the sheriff about Felton?'

She shook her head. 'On nothing but my own say-so? I knew I couldn't get Uncle Dan's support. He wouldn't volunteer that he'd been wrong. Let alone that he'd protected Pelton rather than admit he made a mistake. He might even deny there was ever such a letter.'

For a long while they sat looking at each other. Duff's mind had been jolted so many times, he no longer knew where things stood. At least he understood why Ragan had been so passive under the tremendous threat to his possessions and his life. Why, under the pressure of events, he hid more and more behind the gunmen it had originally been Lois's idea to hire.

He said quietly, 'Why are you leaving, Mandy?'

'I must. I can't stand being here watching it happen. To you.'

He put on his coat and picked up his hat. She stood with her eyes fixed on the glowing draft of the stove. He said, 'So long,' and she didn't answer, and he left.

CHAPTER FOURTEEN

The snow was nearly gone. After a day and night of storm, the dark clouds had vanished, the wind had died. Again the daytime temperature rose high enough to turn the snowpack back into water. It had been winter's warning but not its main assault. The cattle were in good shape, hardly bothered.

The clearing away of the snow left no sign, except for the dead horse, of what had happened at Rock Springs. Duff checked the morning after he and Hob got back from town, nagged by a feeling that there had been more to it than he had supposed.

Sitting his horse at the springs, he tried to put his finger on what troubled him about it. Landers, if Pelton had been right in his identification, had had a pointblank shot at Hob. Yet he had hit the horse, the bullet drilling into its brain, instead of hitting Hob. A man sitting his saddle was a larger, easier-to-hit target than a horse's head.

Duff swung down and walked over to the rock Landers had forted behind and hunkered there, himself. By lining an imaginary rifle on the carcass of Hob's horse, he proved to himself that Landers had had ample time to draw a bead. A man would think he had actually tried to shoot the horse instead of

Hob. And then slip off to his accomplice and get away before Hob got himself untangled. But Landers had felt impelled to take a look at the results, before he left, and Hob had been too quick for him.

And that, Duff suspected, was approximately what had happened. Outright, waylay murder on Hob's home ground would be dangerous. Hob had been too canny to take their, milder bait. So they had made it stronger, a seeming attempt on his life. The real attempt was to have come on Ragan's undisputed property, with Hob on the undisputable offensive.

Duff rode on to where the accomplice had waited for Landers. There wasn't much left there, either, for the horseshoe cuts on what had been frozen ground but now was mushy earth had almost settled out of existence. At the cost of considerable patience, he managed to pick up enough sign to be sure that it led from and back to Ragan's fork. Thereafter he didn't waste time trying to pick his way but rode directly on toward that fork. His direction took him, as he expected, to the head of that creek.

Left with little doubt as to the origin of the mischief, Duff followed a fairly worn trail down onto the bottom. The killing of Landers was being concealed, and that in itself was an extremely serious business. He had no suspicion that Lois knew a thing about it. But a pointed inquiry about her missing new man might make her wonder how much was going on unknown to her. He had barely ridden onto the bottom when a voice behind him ripped out.

'Hold up there, buck!'

Duff reined in, his shoulders drawn tight. Then he risked a shot in the back by swinging the horse around. Tate Peters had stepped out of a brush patch Duff had passed unsuspectingly. Peters had a rifle in his hands, held at the ready. Behind him stood Higbee, who had a six-gun on his hip but whose hands were still empty. There was a look of triumph on their hard-bitten faces. Yet he hadn't needed that to convince him they had been laying in wait for somebody to come along by that route, now that the snow was off the ground. If he had been Hob, he would have been dead by now. This was the rest of the trap they had set, but the wrong man had blundered into it.

The pair advanced toward him in measured steps. Then Peters stopped and gave him a long, hard stare. 'You were told to stay off this spread,' he said in a whiskey voice. 'Maybe you're deaf.'

'I've got business here,' Duff said.

'You've got no business here, or even in the other hollow. Light down.'

The rifle moved menacingly. Duff swung out of the saddle, weighing his chances of reaching his gun before he died. They were close to zero. Peters tipped a nod to Higbee, who came forward and took his gun.

'Now, turn around,' Peters snapped.

Duff obeyed reluctantly. Higbee sprang in, seized his arms and pinned them behind him. He was a powerful man, Duff realized when he found himself swung around to face Peters again. Peters was grinning broadly now. He leaned the rifle against a rock.

'If you don't hear so good,' Peters taunted, 'we'll try another way of getting the idea across.'

Duff braced himself as the man surged toward him. He stiffened his muscles, but it didn't soften the impact of the fists that Peters drove into his belly, his face, or of the knee Peters slammed to his crotch. Staggered and sick, Duff tried to swing himself out of the way. Higbee held him like a vice through another barrage of smashing fists. Duff felt his lip split and blood run across his mouth. He saw crazy lights each time knuckles collided against his eyes. He sagged against Higbee, whose knee booted him erect. He received Peters' knee in the crotch again and, when Higbee abruptly let loose, fell helplessly to the ground.

Even so, Peters stepped over and picked up his rifle, taking no chances. Giving him no chance. They kept his gun and vanished into the brush that had spewed them forth. After a couple of gagging moments, Duff heard their horses leaving. He still couldn't get to his feet.

He didn't know how much later it was when he pushed to a stand and managed to stay erect. His bleeding mouth had splashed his whole front with blood. His punished eyes were puffed already, so he could hardly see. His stomach retched. His crotch was on fire. His horse still there. He saw that they had dropped its reins to hold it. They wanted him to go back to camp because there would be no hiding this from Hob. He managed to swing into the saddle and stay there.

He rode on down the fork toward Ragan's headquarters.

He realized as he drew near that Peters and Higbee had gone there. This didn't deter him for a breath. His head roared, and he hurt all over. But his vision had cleared and he was steady. They hadn't expected him to do anything like this. He rode right up to the house without seeing anybody, although there were several horses in the corral.

He swung down, lurched across the porch and shoved open the door.

They were eating their noon meal. Not only Peters and Higbee. Lois and Dan Ragan sat at the table there. Duff didn't know which of them looked the most surprised when their eyes lifted from their food and riveted on him. Ragan's rocky face didn't change, but his eyes went cold and wary. Lois lifted her hand to her mouth. Peters and Higbee looked a little less triumphant than they had up the hollow.

Lois said feebly, 'What happened to you?'

'Ask your tough hands.'

They hadn't reported it. Ragan cut his eyes to them. Lois also looked at them, puzzled and frowning. Peters set his jaw.

'We caught him sneaking around on our range. Figured he needed a lesson.'

'By throwing down on me from the brush,' Duff added. 'Then by one of them pinning my arms behind me while the other had his fun.'

While that seemed to be news to Ragan, he was ready to back his men. His eyes grew harder yet. 'If you were sneaking around on my range, you had it coming.'

'I was coming here on business,' Duff snapped. 'I told them that. I aimed to inquire about your new gunhand. Landers. Seen him the last day or so?'

'Landers?' Lois's bewilderment was genuine.

Duff wasn't so sure about Ragan, who said frigidly, 'Even if I knew a man named Landers, I wouldn't know what you're driving at.'

It came to Duff that maybe the man didn't. He was far less certain about Higbee and Peters. They were both tense, wary, spoiling and ready for trouble. It reminded Duff that once before he had wondered if they were acting on their own, trying to stir up trouble on both sides.

'If you really don't,' he told Ragan, 'you

better get yourself some new men.'

'His brain's addled,' Higbee snorted. 'Tate hit him too hard.'

Lois's look shut him up. She knew about the steers, supposedly strays, still carrioning off on the plateau. And about the supposedly stray horses that had been brought home, instead of getting the treatment the steer had got.

Duff looked at Tate Peters and said grimly, 'I'll take my gun.'

Peters grinned derisively.

'If you've got his gun,' Lois snapped, 'give it back to him.'

'It's in my saddlebag.'

'Then get it.'

Peters glowered. Then he rose and went out through the back door.

'You, too,' Lois said. 'And no more rough stuff. Hear?' Higbee got up and followed Peters.

Lois studied her plate, then looked up at Duff. 'Supposing you explain what you mean about Landers?'

'He was around and then disappeared. If your dad doesn't know about it, he'd better set himself to finding out.'

Duff swung and walked out. He knew he had gotten somewhere with Lois, and any handicap to the others was a help to himself. He swung up and sat his saddle until Peters and Higbee came across the yard with his gun. As Duff expected, they had unloaded it. That didn't matter. What he wanted was the weapon. He could tell from their eyes that he would do well to keep it handy from there on.

'Any time you lobos feel lucky enough to try it alone,' he said, 'come around.'

He rode straight for the cow camp on the other branch. He was all but convinced that someone besides Ragan was directing the activities of that pair. Somebody who had got to them and put them on a second payroll. Someone who wanted Ragan off his mind and for Hob to kill him.

But he still couldn't tell Hob that. It would give Hob another man to kill, his treacherous friend as well as his ancient enemy.

Hob was waiting at the camp, grown uneasy because he hadn't shown up to eat. Duff rode straight to the corral and took care of his horse, dreading their meeting. He found Hob putting food on the table. Hob took his first good look at him and widened his eyes.

'What in hell happened to you?'

'Horse slipped and throwed me,' Duff said. 'Spang into a rock.'

'Face first?'

'Don't it look like it?'

Hob said nothing while Duff took off his bloody coat, then tried to wash his wrecked face. His ribs ached, and his belly was a stiff, sore slab. He almost groaned aloud when he sat down at the table. He had no appetite, but he reached for the stew.

'All right,' Hob said. 'What other comical ways can you explain it?'

'I strayed into the north hollow and got jumped. By Peters and Higbee.'

'I knew it.' Hob's face went black. 'The minute I seen you.'

'Well, hold onto your temper. We were warned to stay away from there. I was trespassing.'

'Why?

'I guess curiosity got the best of me.'

'What did you do to them?'

'Best I could. There were two of them.'

Hob said fumingly, 'By God, we'll teach 'em!'

'Whoa, there. That's exactly why they sent me home looking like this. I thought at first they're trying to bait you into a trap where you're dead in the wrong and they can kill you and hope to get away with it. Now I think it's Ragan they want killed, and they're trying to goose you into losing your head and doing it for them. I think that's what Landers, if that was his name, was trying for at Rock Springs. I checked it, this morning. He could have killed you easy, if that had been his intention.'

'You're out of your head,' Hob retorted. 'Why would *they* want me to kill Ragan?'

'I dunno,' Duff lied. 'Just see you don't take this new bait and bust over there breathing fire.'

'I told you at Pike's. When I kill Ragan, he'll

165

be coming for me, not the other way around. I'm no damned fool. I'm as anxious as you are to keep my neck out of a noose.'

'Dead man's poker. He baits you, and you bait him, till somebody goes wild and starts it.'

'He's a lot jumpier than I am.'

Duff shook his head. 'This is the second time you've admitted your intention to kill him. How come you weren't this open about Mounts and Fleeson?'

Hob pushed back in his chair. 'So you still think I killed them.'

'I'd like to be certain you didn't.'

'Mounts fell off a bridge. Fleeson hung himself.' Hob seemed really to believe that.

It hit Duff like a mule kick. Maybe Pelton had been the killer, in their cases. With Hob set up to be the goat, as his father had been, if something happened to throw the fat in the fire.

'But you're going to kill Ragan. Why did you decide that? And when?'

Hob scowled. 'He passed the death sentence on Burley.'

'I don't think you had special plans for Ragan when you first come here,' Duff retorted. 'It turned out they won't cringe and crawl and run to hide. Especially Lois. She called your bluff. Now you've got to make good on those threats she laughed at you about'

'Don't talk to me about her,' Hob snapped.

'I'm trying to talk sense into you. Don't do it. Not when you've got no idea what you're really doing.'

Hob didn't answer him.

CHAPTER FIFTEEN

Duff opened his eyes to be reminded of his awakening the morning after he and Hob visited the honkytonk across the river from Dalles City. Except that this time the misery was all on the surface of his body. His eyes were hot and nearly closed. His lips felt like those of a moose. His belly was still rigid with soreness, and he wondered if Tate Peters had cracked a rib. He turned over with a stifled groan because of Hob in the other bunk and stared into the darkness. The days were at their shortest, now, and he always woke up before dawn. It was the second time in his life, that he could remember, when he hated to get out of bed.

His anger, which he had carefully bridled because of Hob, was hard to hold back in the privacy of the darkness. No man could take the helpless beating he had taken and not want to do something about it. His outrage was all the greater because of his conviction that Lois, like himself, had had something put over on her. But he had shaken her complacency about it, finally.

He sat up, threw his legs over the edge of the bunk and stood up, slowly, stiffly and painfully. He was always up ahead of Hob, and he didn't light the lamp. Moving quietly, he fed kindling and wood into the stove and got a fire started. Light leaked out as the fire grew, and he was dressing by it when he turned his head to look at Hob and didn't see him.

Hob's bunk was empty.

For a moment Duff stood with one leg shoved into his pants. Then he finished putting on the pants, struck another match and touched it to the cold wick of the lamp. His heart drummed in his chest. He didn't really need to look to see that the rifle was gone from its place beside the door. He pulled his shirt on over his head, put on his socks and boots. It wouldn't be light for another hour. But he didn't know what he could do, even if it were light now.

He poured himself coffee and rolled one of his infrequent cigarettes. The coffee stung his mouth and gums, but the smoke was comforting. Why did he keep bucking the situation when at every turn he was blocked by mystery? All it had produced so far was lost ground. And he knew as well as he knew anything that another grim turn of events had come. Touched off by yesterday's beating.

He coaxed coffee past the bruises and cuts until he had emptied the cup. He rolled another cigarette, the thought of food still unattractive. When first light seeped through the window, he put on his stained sheepskin and his hat. He took down the box of shells from the shelf and reloaded his six-gun. It was no surprise to find that Hob's saddle was gone from its pole, his favorite horse from the corral.

The earth, frozen and then mushy, had become firm enough again to hold sign. He didn't waste time hunting it, there where there was too much of it around. He knew the direction Hob had taken and the quickest way to get to the north fork. A little later, with the light grown strong, he was following an open stitching of new horse tracks. They led across Ragan's half of the plateau. They dropped to the bottom and there turned up the hollow.

Duff didn't follow beyond that point. At that time of day, Hob wasn't apt to run into trouble, whatever new trouble he intended to make. Somewhat relieved to know that he hadn't headed straight for the horse ranch headquarters, Duff rode back to high ground and worked his way to where he could see Ragan's buildings. The occupants were stirring. Smoke rose from the house chimney. While he watched he saw two men come out of the barn. They would be Peters and Higbee. They probably bunked in the barn and took their meals at the house.

He watched them cross to the house. He wondered if Ragan was still there and hoped he was. It bothered him, as it had once bothered Hob, to have Lois living more or less alone with that pair. If they ever turned on her, she would be no match for them, spunky

170

and dominating as she was.

Seeing no point in courting more trouble, Duff started back to the cow camp. He reached it to find Hob there ahead of him, serenely making breakfast.

'Where've you been so early?' Hob asked, when Duff stepped into the dugout.

'That won't keep me from asking you the same question,' Duff snapped.

'I thought I heard a calf bellering. Made me think of timber wolves. Cold as it's been, they'll be down from the mountains hungry, if they're not here already.'

'Why didn't you rouse me?'

'Shape you're in, figured you needed your sleep.'

'Find the calf?'

Hob shook his head. 'No sign of anything.'

'So tell me where you really were.'

Hob grinned. He was in high spirits. 'Was that any sillier than your yarn about being thrown off your horse face first?'

'What were you doing in the north hollow?'

'Looking around. Figured you trailed me there.'

'Far enough.' Apparently Hob hadn't stayed there long and had come back a different way. Duff shrugged, for Hob was slithering out from under the questions. 'But I wish you'd get it through your head. Neither one of us knows what all is going on. Get yourself caught over there, and you might find yourself in

171

something you never bargained for.'

'Did I get caught?'

'Keep crowding your luck, and you will.'

Duff managed to eat breakfast, although it was a painful job. He didn't believe for a minute that Hob had sneaked off well before daylight just to look around. Darkness was hardly the time for that. Maybe he had chosen it to avoid an encounter over there. Possibly he had hoped to get back in time to escape being found out. Duff had a deep, intuitive fear that he had started something cooked up between himself and Pelton, the other night in town. Something he might only have been considering until the beating suffered by his partner triggered him into action on it.

Hob finished a cigarette and said cheerily, 'You're not up to riding, today. No reason you should. The way the stuff's bunched, these days, I can cover everything that needs it.'

Duff glanced at him suspiciously. He was beginning to distrust every suggestion Hob made. But he hadn't been looking forward to spending several hours in the saddle. The ride Hob had forced on him, that morning, had been uncomfortable, and he was still wondering about a cracked rib.

'Maybe I'll let you,' he said with reluctance. 'For today.'

'I'm not looking for more trouble,' Hob said, aware of his uneasiness. 'Like I told you. If it finds me, it'll have to come looking for me.'

Relieved, Duff watched him saddle his horse and ride out again. He went off across the bottom, as he had done on many another morning. Duff stretched out on the bunk again, glad of the chance to take it easy. In that position his side didn't hurt, and he even managed to put his worry out of his mind. Drowsiness began to build in him, and he let it take him.

When he woke up again he felt pretty much restored, still stiff but not so sore. Then he sat up, for a glance at the clock told him it was nearly noon. Hob would be in soon to eat. The fire in the stove had gone out, and Duff built another. He needed a fresh pail of water and had stepped out to go to the spring when he saw the rider coming.

The rider wasn't Hob, and he came from toward the north fork.

Duff got the water and carried it into the dugout. He was standing in the doorway when the oncomer enlarged enough to tell him it was Dan Ragan. Bewildered, Duff could only wonder and worry. Ragan had avoided them like poison so far. He had tough men he could have brought along to safeguard him, this time. But, Duff saw when Ragan came on in to the camp, he wasn't even armed.

Yet his set, heavy face was stained with anger. Duff remembered fleetingly what Hob had said before he left, 'If trouble finds me, it'll have to come looking for me.' Yet if he had expected this, he would surely have been here, himself, instead of leaving his partner behind. Unless, Duff reflected, he hadn't expected anyone to be over from the horse ranch so soon.

'Who done it?' Ragan demanded, his voice heavy and rough. 'You or Loman?'

'Did what?'

Duff was mystified enough to convince Ragan that he didn't understand. The man said, with only slightly less belligerence, 'I didn't think it was you. Although it looked like a thing a man might do, after what happened to you yesterday. Where's Loman?'

'He'll be here to eat, pretty soon.'

'I'll wait for him.'

'But what's wrong?'

'What's wrong?' Ragan said explosively. 'I'm just out the best blooded stallion ever brought into this country. Drove all the way from Kentucky and cost me a mint. The only stud I had or would let run with my mares.'

Duff glimpsed the truth, although most of it was still clogged in Ragan's throat. He remembered the animal, a beauty he had once seen over there. He understood Hob's morning ride, the rifle he had taken along. Hob had located the stallion in the predawn darkness but had been obliged to wait for light to make sure of a good shot. The viciousness, the very waste of it appalled Duff as it had

174

outraged Ragan.

'All I can say about it,' he said weakly, 'is that it's news to me.'

'Maybe so.' Ragan eyed him. 'I peg you a notch above Loman. But only a notch.'

Duff withdrew into the dugout, his head still reeling. He couldn't credit Hob's doing as cruel and senseless a thing as that. Yet it hadn't seemed senseless to Hob. It had had a purpose. It had been a blow stinging enough to bring Ragan here on the warpath. It had cut the vital heart out of what ranch the man had left, with half of Dutch Hollow as good as lost to him. Without a sire, his brood herd would run barren. It would be ages before the blooded animal could be replaced from the East, even if Ragan could get up the money for it.

Now Ragan was here breathing fire, another thing Hob had wanted. But Ragan had come unarmed, or armed only with a courage even Duff hadn't thought he possessed. Duff wished they could talk about it, get to the bottom of things and try to straighten it all out. He glanced out the window to see Ragan staring up the hollow. Hob was coming in to noon. Duff went back to the doorway and stepped out. Ragan flicked him a glance. Hob was still a small shape in the distance.

'Ragan,' Duff said quickly, 'it might not be too late. Bend your neck for once, and go to Brig Langford about that letter.'

Ragan swung his head, his eyes wide and startled. But he rode it out and said curtly, 'So Mandy told you about that foolishness.'

'It wasn't foolishness. I don't think so. She don't. And you don't, either.'

'There wasn't a thing to it.' Ragan's mind had closed again like a steel trap.

Duff hit him again just as hard. 'Pelton's behind all this. He's meddled with your men. They're working for him, not you. I tried to warn you yesterday.'

The man was as unshakable as bedrock. 'You nearly had Lois believing it. Till this morning, when she heard what happened to the stud. Don't try to tell me my men did that.'

There was no time to tell him Felton was using Hob, also. Hob had recognized Ragan and lifted his horse to a trot. He came in with the ghost of a grin on his mouth. The discovery that Ragan was unarmed wiped it out. For a long moment they sat their saddles and held each other's hostile eyes.

'I'd have come with the sheriff,' Ragan said, finally. 'Except that Doncaster would lie you into the clear again. I warned you to leave me and mine alone. You paid no heed. I figured to let you stay here till spring. Now you can clear out, winter or no winter, or be run out.'

Ragan turned his back on them and rode away.

Ignoring Hob, Duff went back into the dugout. Hob went over to the corral to take

176

care of his horse. He was sober-faced when he came in, and he washed up in silence.

'Well,' he said with a nervous laugh, when he came over and sat down at the table. 'The old boy's got a little sand in his craw, at that.'

'And more brains in his head,' Duff snapped, 'than you've got in yours. He knew you hit him that stinking low blow to bring him over here, finally. And he was smart enough to come unarmed.' It was the wrong kind of thing to say to Hob, but Duff couldn't help it. 'Oh, you've got cunning, all right. Even if it didn't bring you your chance to kill him and claim self-defense, you showed him again he can't run a horse ranch next door to you. Helped to convince him he'd do better letting you take over the whole hollow. Only, he doesn't intend for it to come out, that way. Looks like you're going to find yourself trying to hold onto the south fork, even.'

'Me?' Hob looked up from his plate of beans. 'You pulling out of it?'

'What difference would it make to you? Your real partner is Pike Pelton.'

Hob's mouth dropped open. He stopped eating. 'What made you say that?'

'You couldn't have shot down a fine horse like that unless you were egged into it. I think Pelton suggested it. But you couldn't bring yourself to it till I got beat up, over there.'

Hob averted his eyes. That was all the proof Duff needed.

But it still hadn't got Ragan killed, Duff thought bitterly. So something even worse would have to be done to bring it off.

CHAPTER SIXTEEN

Lois felt a leaden weight in her heart while she watched her father ride off toward Dalles City in the early morning light. She knew he hated to leave her there now. For the same reason, she hated to see him go. But Hob Loman, however shrewdly he had judged it, hadn't begun to guess the heavy blow he had dealt.

Ever since they came to Dalles City, and he set himself up as a horse trader, Dan Ragan had operated on a frayed shoestring. Initially this had consisted of buying horses in the Willamette, or from valley farmers who brought them over the mountains to sell. And then trying to turn a profit on them locally or along the upper river and even in the mining camps. Sometime it had been profitable, and again just the opposite. Such money as he had got ahead, he had put into the ranch. So far he had sold little out of his own horse band, which he had been trying to grade up in blood. The filly colts were to be used for breeding mares, after they had matured. The increase hadn't yet become large enough for there to be many geldings to sell.

And now there would be no increase, at all, until there was a new blooded sire.

So the pressure of necessity had forced him to leave the ranch once more. Every dime he could scrape up would be needed. He was even talking about putting the town house up for sale. Then he could order another stallion from Kentucky, to be delivered the earliest possible in the summer to come.

Meanwhile, they had to meet the payroll Hob Loman had forced on them. Peters and Higbee would have to be kept on, now, or somebody in their place. Her father had set his mind to remove the threat to the ranch, even if he had to hire yet more men to do it. Lois had agreed as to the necessity of that. They couldn't go on the way things had been all fall. The beautiful animal lying up there in the hollow proved that.

When her father was out of sight, Lois dropped the window curtain and turned back into the room. It was a pleasant room. Like Mandy, she was a natural housekeeper who had never been allowed much of it. She went to the kitchen, which she had yet to straighten up after the breakfast she had served the three men. She was glad the hired men had already ridden out on the day's work. They were under stern orders from her father, as well as from herself, never to do anything on their own hook again. But she no longer had the confidence she had once felt in her control of them.

The doubts had begun to appear the day Duff Doncaster brought home the stray horses. Try as she would, she couldn't hate

180

Duff with the unshakable animosity she felt toward Hob Loman. There was a gentleness in Duff that reached her at the most awkward moments. Yet he was no limp rag. He had troubled to bring home the horses, but he had told her in grim-mouthed annoyance about the three steers of theirs somebody had killed.

She remembered how she had flared up, saying, 'Are you accusing *me* of shooting them?'

And he had said, 'No, but I think one of your men did . . . After hazing them where they had a flimsy excuse.' Then he had said that the men were bad medicine. That Hob Loman, of all people, worried about her living pretty much alone with them. She had felt Duff's concern, at least, to be genuine.

Later she had checked on the steers, herself, and found the situation to be in line with Duff's description. Yet Peters and Higbee, when she confronted them, had flatly denied any part in or knowledge of it.

'That's a trick,' Peters had scoffed. 'They drove the steers over the deadline, theirselves, and shot 'em.'

'Then why didn't they shoot the stray horses?'

'Likely they weren't strays at all,' Higbee offered. 'Doncaster picked 'em up on our range and drove 'em in to throw you off guard.'

She had let herself believe that because she

181

had wanted to believe it.

But that incident had been nothing like the other day when Duff walked in on them so horribly beaten up she had nearly fainted. There had been something magnificent in the way he had come in, after what they had done to him, and in the way he had demanded and got back his six-gun. From that moment on she had known what Mandy saw in him. What Mandy loved in him. She had felt so sorry for them and for what was happening to Duff because of his blind loyalty to a man like Hob Loman.

Yet in a way she could understand that in Duff. When Hob was a boy and herself only a silly girl she had been drawn to him powerfully. A more physical thing than Mandy's feeling for Duff, for she was enough older than Mandy to make the difference. Hob had had something that made her heartbeat quicken and her cheeks grow warm. While Duff's response was different he felt the magnetism she once felt. An animal magnetism, there maybe because he had danger built into him. There had been girls in the wagon train who thought Burley Loman was a very attractive man.

Lois shook off her mood of sadness, thinking again of Duff's defiance of Peters and Higbee, even after what they had done to him. That same evening, when they were alone in the house and the men in the bunk room in

182

the barn, she had had one of her rare arguments with her father. That beating had been cowardly and inexcusable, as he had agreed. But he had tried to excuse it, anyway, by saying the men had got carried away in obeying their orders to protect the ranch and everything pertaining to it. He had denied any understanding of Duff's reference to someone named Landers.

Dan Ragan was no liar, and she had believed him. Yet she had insisted that he pay the men off and get rid of them. They could get along without such help, or at least hire replacements they knew they could trust. As a woman, she had always been afraid of them in spite of the cool, impersonal relationship she had managed to maintain. Peters was the worse, the younger of the two men, and more than once she had caught him eying her.

That had been more effective on her father than the other factors. But he hadn't wanted to let them go until he had lined up replacements. The next forenoon they had found the shot stallion. That had changed everything back the way it had been at the start, as far as her feelings were concerned. It had worsened them materially. The maliciousness had been a crippling blow to the ranch, even graver than the threatened loss of the south hollow which wasn't presently needed. And now her father, driven to the end of his patience, had declared his intention of driving them out.

She had admired him for the way he had delivered his final warning. Neither of them had believed that Duff had killed the stallion in retaliation for the beating. It had had to be Hob, using that as an excuse to strike back, low and hard. It had been intended to bring Dan Ragan smoking and give Hob Loman ostensible grounds for his third murder. The hangman, the witness—and now the judge. Her father had come awfully close to obliging him. She had never seen him so shaken out of his iron-willed self-command. But the command had prevailed. Peters and Higbee had been more than eager to go to the cow camp with him and have it out, then and there. He had told them sternly to keep out of it and had gone to the camp alone, shrewdly denying Hob Loman his grounds.

When she had finished her morning housework, Lois found herself too restless to stay close to headquarters, the way her father had instructed. Intimidation had never worked with her, and she had little taste for allowing Peters and Higbee the run of the outdoors while she stayed timidly home. Her saddle was equipped with a boot, and she always rode with a rifle in it. Graded-up young horses were a tempting prize for vagrant thieves. There were animal predators to guard against, too. She changed to riding clothes, which in her case had always been a boy's shirt and pants.

She pulled on her boots, the pant legs tucked in. She put on a heavy, short coat and her riding hat.

She had never liked the feeling she got from changing her sex through changing her wrappings. But she should have been born a boy, unattractive to men and immune to them. She had always felt that her father wished it had been that way. At least she had always felt a need to try to act like a boy, she thought while she saddled Rusty at the corral. Holding the girl things and then the woman things that she liked to a minimum.

The hired men had ridden up the branch, so she struck out in the opposite direction. This also would keep her from stumbling onto the dead stallion, which she hadn't seen and couldn't bear to think about. For a while she rode swiftly, letting Rusty stretch out. He was small but tough and wiry, and she had raised and trained him from a colt. She reached the fork of the two creeks and, just below, stopped to let him blow and to draw in the clean, cold air, herself.

She had been there only a few minutes when she heard the hit of the hoofs of a fast-moving horse. The sound came from on down the creek. Not wanting to meet anyone, she swung Rusty into the brush and stepped down. She stood at his head to keep him quiet while the horse and rider came on. In another moment her breath caught, and she was glad she had avoided contact.

The rider was Pike Pelton.

He passed her unknowingly and rode on. She expected him to turn up the southfork, on his way to visit his cronies at the cow camp. To her surprise, he veered to the left and entered the north fork. She watched him bewilderedly, for he had no business in that hollow. Frowning, she swung onto Rusty's back and began to follow. She would have detested Pelton even without his defense of Burley Loman and his attitude toward her people ever since. If for some reason he was going to the house, she was glad she hadn't stayed there. Yet she kept following him, keeping back a cautious distance.

Less than a third of the way to headquarters, Pelton puzzled her again by leaving the bottom and turning onto the southside plateau, the one between the two creek branches. It warned her instantly that he was up to no good purpose. A rope seemed to have been coiled around her chest and pulled tight, but she kept after him stubbornly. Though rough and climbing, the country was fairly open, but he seemed to have no inkling that there was someone behind him. He rode steadily, showing a familiarity with the region that deepened her concern. He topped out on the plateau and ahead was a local landmark of broken buttes.

She had almost ridden into view behind him

when she saw the two men waiting ahead of Pelton at the landmark. A rendezvous at a place easy to describe. She cut off behind some rocks, sure that the waiting men were Duff and Hob Loman. Her heart was like a wild pigeon in her chest. Something new was afoot, although she couldn't fathom why Pelton was taking a personal hand in it.

She swung down, trailed reins, and drew the rifle from its boot. Rusty could be depended on to wait there for her, no matter what happened. Afoot, the cover was a greater help to her. She slipped forward swiftly, darting from brush clump to rock crop. When she dared to take a look, she found herself practically on top of them. And she stood half-paralyzed.

The men who had been waiting for Pelton were Peters and Higbee.

Pelton had swung down, too. They were talking earnestly, although she couldn't hear what they said. But the fear that had ridden with her from the forks had changed to anger. She crept on. When she stepped into view, her rifle was at the ready and pointed squarely at Pelton's chest.

Peters was the first to see her. His back straightened, and he said something from the side of his mouth. Pelton glanced at him, then turned his head. Higbee swung to look, too, then stood there staring.

'Why, Miss Lois.' Pelton touched his hat to

her mockingly. 'You could scare a man to death popping up like that.'

'You'll be worse than scared,' Lois said angrily. 'Unless there's a good reason for this.'

'Reason for what?' Pelton asked innocently.

'You coming here to see these men on the sly.'

'Why, I was just riding through. This is a shortcut I take sometimes, when I'm on my way to the John Day. Met up with these boys, and we stopped to chew the fat. That's all.'

'It's not all by a lot. Duff Doncaster was right.'

Pelton pricked up his ears. 'Duff? About what?'

Lois knew at once that she shouldn't have mentioned Duff. Peters and Higbee were watching Pelton intently, their eyes gone hard. She ignored his question and spoke to them.

'You two get riding. You can look up my father in town for your money.' She didn't want them returning to head-quarters now and added, 'Never mind your personals. I'll send them in.'

They hadn't expected that from her, and she was afraid they would erupt then and there. Pelton's face darkened, but he was still trying to throw dust in her eyes. 'Now, Miss Lois,' he objected. 'There's no call for that. If I kept these boys from their work, it's my fault, not their'n. I like to jower.'

'And cook up mischief,' Lois snapped. The

change in Pelton's eyes didn't deter her. She had stumbled onto something that made the situation graver even than she had thought. She was frightened again but too angry to betray it. 'You two are through. Get out of Dutch Hollow and don't ever show yourselves around here again.'

They glanced at Pelton. Almost imperceptibly, he nodded his head. They mounted and rode off along the plateau toward the forks. Her heart jumped in her chest when she remembered that Rusty was off in that direction. But if they tried to haze him away and leave her afoot, he wouldn't go far and would come at her whistle. She stepped around so she could watch them out of sight and yet keep an eye on Pelton. He was an angry man now, upset and dangerous. When she was sure the others would really leave, she gave him her attention again.

He said with thinly veiled malice, 'What've you been hearing from Duff Doncaster?'

She should have bitten off her tongue before she dragged Duff into it, but it was too late now. She said, 'Enough. And what I told them goes for you. Get riding. And keep off this range.'

He turned to his horse and swung up. He eyed her again, then rode eastward. He was carrying out his pretense of only having been passing through Dutch Hollow.

Panic hit her when she realized what she

might have brought on herself, the ranch, and even Duff. Peters and Higbee were traitors and might have been from the day she hired them. She made her way back to Rusty. They hadn't bothered him. She had broken up their game, and they were going to town. They would want the money they had coming to them. Whether or not they told her father why they had left their jobs, he would know something was wrong and return immediately.

She rode directly down to the bottom and in another ten minutes was home. She gave Rusty water, unsaddled and wiped him down, then turned him back into the corral. She went into the house through the back door, and there at the kitchen table sat Tate Peters.

She said heavily, hoarsely, 'Get out!'

He grinned at her. 'Why, Miss Lois. You ain't my boss any longer. So there's no reason I shouldn't come courting you.'

'I said get out!'

She tried to swing up the rifle she had brought to the house, where she always kept it when she was there. He sprang forward and knocked it aside. He grabbed the barrel and wrenched the weapon from her hands. He tossed it aside and seized and pulled her into his arms. She nearly fainted, yet her muscles reacted in outrage. She clawed and kicked and wrenched, yet he tugged her tighter to him. She managed to turn her head so he couldn't reach her mouth. He kissed her on the ear, then pushed her off with a savage shove.

'Fun later,' he said. 'But don't worry. I don't aim to neglect you. I been waiting a long time for it.'

She darted toward the rifle he had let fall to the floor. He gave her another push, so rough she fell. He picked up the rifle and unloaded it, dropping the shells into the pocket of his coat. It was the only gun on the place besides the six-gun he wore on his hip. Her predicament hit her hard. If they weren't going to town, there was no hope of her father's hurrying back.

She looked up at Peters and said falteringly, 'What are you waiting for?'

'Just you be patient.' His grin was lewd and brutish. 'You upset Pike's wagon up there. It's making him scramble getting it fixed.'

Lois got to her feet, her guess as to Pelton's corrective measures stabbing fear into her again. They thought she knew more than she actually did know, with Duff the source of her information. She wished she did know what all he knew or guessed. There had been his mysterious reference to a man named Landers, who had been around and then disappeared. And other things to make this as deadly as she sensed it to be.

Peters was waiting for something, but he hadn't lost interest in her as a woman. He sat down at the table again and let his eyes strip her out of the boy clothes.

191

'You might give a man some coffee,' he said.

She went to the stove. He swiveled in his chair so she couldn't get behind him. His eyes terrified her. Her own looked longingly at the door. It was too far away to reach, even if it would do her any good to escape the house. Whatever else he intended, they were going to kill her. He would shoot her before she could reach the corral and Rusty.

The fire was out, the coffee cold. She said, 'You want it hot?'

'Sure I want it hot.'

She laid kindling and set a match to it. Something burned in his eyes that warned her he might not wait. She shoved in more wood and pulled the coffee pot forward. Anything to keep him from grabbing her.

CHAPTER SEVENTEEN

Duff was on the eastern end of the plateau. It lacked an hour of midday, and he had swung south to head for camp to eat when he saw the smoke that towered into the cold sky to the west. He reined in, his mouth ajar, and put a hard stare on the weaving plume. It was too far south to be lifting from Ragan's hollow, his first thought. When he got his bearings, he went pounding down the broken slope to the bottom.

He could still see the smoke from down there, growing heavier, frayed by the wind but too dense to be torn apart. By then he was sure of the source, and he rode with grim purpose. Cattle were scattered along to his left, and his rushing passage spooked some of them, but he paid no heed. He was soon close enough to see, far ahead, the springfed grove of trees that sheltered the cow camp. He could see that the upper body of smoke had two spark-streaked roots at the bottom.

He drove his horse at breakneck speed, while knowing it was too late to save the camp. Dan Ragan had begun the job of clearing out the south fork. When he whipped in on the burning dugout and barn, they were far gone. The spare horses whistled and plunged wildly against the pole rails of the corral. He threw himself from the saddle, raced to the gate and opened it. The horses went galloping past him and down the hollow. He hauled himself around and saw that be couldn't get into the dugout. Everything inside was on fire.

Hob was somewhere off to the south, or should have been. There was almost no chance that he had returned early and been caught inside, maybe shot by whoever had set the fires. Duff scorched his face trying to see inside, but he could see nothing. He couldn't even get to the water bucket. Wheeling, he raced to the spring and pulled off his hat. It wouldn't do the slightest good, yet he scooped up a hatful of water. He ran with it to the dugout door and sloshed the smoking door frame. The water dampered the flames for a second or so, but he still could make out nothing inside. He turned and ran back to the spring.

He had just straightened to rush to the dugout with more water when a voice sang out behind him.

'You ain't going to spoil that pretty fire, are you, man?'

Duff spun around. Roscoe Higbee had stepped from behind the trunk of one of the larger trees. He had a six-gun gripped tightly. His eyes were gleaming.

'You son of a bitch,' Duff growled.

'Hey, now. Talk nice. You and me are taking a ride together.'

194

'The hell we are.'

'No?'

The gun exploded. The hat Duff held began to spurt water on two sides. Two inches over, and the bullet would have drilled his chest.

'If you want to wear it a while yet, put it on,' Higbee ordered. 'Then pluck that six-shooter and drop it, peaceful.'

Duff saw murder in the eyes above the smirking mouth. He lifted his gun from its holster, fighting the urge to try his luck. It would be suicide. Giving in might also be, but it might give him some kind of a break. Higbee made him back off, then stepped forward and quickly scooped up the gun.

'My horse is down a piece,' he said, nodding west. 'We'll pick up yours and have us a look at the country together.'

Duff growled, 'Where's my pardner?'

'Don't recollect seeing him, lately.'

That could be true or untrue, but if Hob was inside that burning soddy there was nothing that could be done for him now.

When they both had horses under them, Higbee headed him onto the plateau. They were going to Ragan's headquarters, although Duff couldn't see why he should be taken there. Ragan had lost no time after delivering his threat to clear out the south fork. The camp was gone already. The next step would be to move out the cattle. Duff couldn't believe Ragan would authorize the killing of

Hob, let alone himself. But Higbee and his sidekick weren't getting all their orders from Ragan.

Higbee hurried him. He didn't seem to care that they were leaving easy-to-read tracks. That left Duff with only a flickering hope that Hob was still alive. Once on the north bottom, Higbee struck directly toward the horse ranch headquarters. Everything there looked quiet. They reached the house, and Higbee watched cautiously while he obeyed the man and swung down.

Higbee dismounted and said, 'Go on in the house.'

Duff pushed open the door and hauled up in surprise. Tate Peters sat at the kitchen table. Cigarette stubs thrown carelessly on the floor suggested that he had been there for some time. Lois sat on the other side of the table, looking pale and frightened. She stared at Duff with a stricken face that told him her part in this was involuntary.

Peters grinned in satisfaction. *'Bueno.* Did you send up the smoke signal?'

'Sure did,' Higbee said with a laugh. 'It's all cinders, now.'

'Muy bueno.'

Lois lifted her head. 'Who's doing this?' she asked Peters. 'You didn't have time to see Pelton after I fired you.'

'Didn't need to see him again,' Peters said. 'This was all set up when you busted out of the

196

brush waving your little popgun. You only gave it the go-ahead.'

She slumped back into abject misery.

Duff said, 'Lois, where's your father?'

'Town,' she said, in an all-gone voice.

'He'll be here pretty soon,' Peters said. 'This is gonna be a real get-together.'

'He doesn't now anything about this, Duff,' Lois said, realizing how it looked to him. 'I caught these men meeting Pike Pelton in secret. I fired them. When I got back to the house, Peters was laying in wait for me.' She glanced at Peters, and her resentment flared. 'How do you intend to trick my father into this, too?'

'He'll come. We'll nail him.'

Higbee poured himself coffee. He had taken off his coat, as Peters had, but they both still wore their hats. Peters rolled another cigarette. Their lack of hurry told Duff they were only waiting for Ragan to get there, however they were summoning him. And then—

Without fully understanding it, he could put some of the pieces in place. Ragan's refusal to let himself be baited, after the shooting of the stallion, had forced a change of plans. Lois's catching Pelton red-handed with these men had forced another change or rushed them. Pelton's sole stake in it was to cover up his guilty past. Somehow he had learned that Ragan wasn't the only one who knew the truth. Duff hoped he hadn't learned that Mandy knew something of it, too.

It was still hard to believe Pelton would take such bloody steps solely because of the past. There was nothing to connect him with the death of Amos Bickle but hearsay and circumstantial evidence. That couldn't be the whole of it. Pelton was frightened by something so recent, so fresh it could be his ruin once suspicion had been centered on him.

It removed Duff's last doubt about who had killed Vince Mounts and Frank Fleeson. It was small comfort to him. Hob still stood to be made the goat, if he was still alive.

Duff watched the two henchmen with cautious eyes. He would get one slim chance, if even that, and now wasn't the time. Higbee was drinking coffee, but he stood well away. Duff had holes in his hat to testify to the man's handiness with the gun again on his hip. Peters was playing amused eyes on Lois. The only time hers weren't filled with hate was when she glanced at Duff. He wondered with a sick stomach what had happened here between them before he and Higbee arrived.

'I'm going to take this coat off,' Duff said. 'It's damned hot in here with it on.'

Peters didn't seem concerned about his comfort. He merely shrugged. They watched warily while he took off the coat, which he tossed into a corner. He tossed the hat after it. He swung quickly toward the table, and they were as ready as he had expected. Higbee's gun was in his hand almost before Duff moved.

'Any reason why I can't set down?' Duff asked.

'Not at the table,' Peters rapped.

That would put him too close to them. Duff pulled a chair well back and sat down. He felt less encumbered with the coat off, but as helpless as before. They were giving him no chance to try anything.

There was another edgy wait, but in this one Peters kept glancing at the kitchen clock. Presently he got up and put on his coat. He picked up the rifle leaning against the wall by the chair he had left. He took cartridges from his coat pocket and began to stuff them into the magazine. Higbee put on his own coat.

'Look in that drawer,' Peters told him. 'She's got kitchen knives.'

'Yeah.'

Higbee pulled open a drawer in the work table by the sink. He took out two butcher knives and a smaller, paring knife. Lois seemed close to wild. She must have placed some feeble hope in the knives. Just as Duff had nursed the slim hope that Hob was still alive and free somewhere. Higbee took the knives with him when he went outside.

Reminded of Hob, Duff's hope mounted slightly. It was past noon. By now, if he still lived, Hob would have discovered the burned camp. He would know who had done it, see it

199

as Duff had at first, as the first step in carrying out Ragan's threat to clear the south fork. His immediate concern would be for his partner. He would spend his first efforts trying to find what had happened to him. When he had exhausted more immediate possibilities, it would occur to him to investigate the horse ranch. These two men intended to be set for him, if he showed, as well as for Ragan.

Duff tried a shot in the dark, saying, 'How do you figure to hang all this on Hob Loman, Peters?'

The man glanced at him, surprised. He didn't answer, but Duff was sure that Hob was still alive. Lois looked curious but not encouraged. She still thought Hob was on their side.

Peters snapped, 'We'll be kitty-cornered to the house, so we can watch all sides. You'll live longer just sitting here, nice and quiet.' He followed Higbee outside.

'You all right, Lois?' Duff asked quietly.

She nodded. 'So far. But I gathered that I'm to be the last to die.' She told him all about it. 'I didn't mean to drag you into it. I'd done it before I realized the consequences.'

'It makes no difference,' Duff said. 'I aimed to brace Pelton and get to the bottom of it. I was only waiting for an excuse to go to town by myself.'

'What did you mean about it being Pelton's second frame job?'

Mandy had told him that Lois knew nothing about the fatal letter. He explained it, watching her face change from disbelief to shock to dismay.

'My father protected Pelton?' she gasped.

'He had to, if he was to protect his own beliefs.'

'Oh, God. If Hob had known that, he might not have done all he has.'

'He'd only have added Pelton to the list. That's why I couldn't tell him. But I'd bet my life the only thing *he's* done was to shoot your stallion.'

'You mean,' Lois gasped, 'that Pelton killed Vince and Uncle Frank?'

'I'd bet my life on that, too.'

Lois looked stunned, left without a thing to hate Hob for except the horse that had become a pawn in the dirty game. He wanted to balance even that. So he told her about the ambush at Rock Springs. And, now, the destruction of their camp. She was silent for a long moment, pale and drawn.

'It makes no difference now,' she said, at last.

'It makes a difference for you to know the truth.'

She nodded her head. 'Yes. It makes a lot of difference. Can't we warn him, somehow?'

'You sure there isn't some kind of weapon around they didn't think of?'

'I don't know of anything.'

Duff searched the house, anyway. There was nothing anywhere near equal to the situation they were caught in. The only hope was that Hob would be too wily to fall into the trap. Pacing the floor, Duff remembered how Mandy had once charged that Hob had let him down and would again. Yet, just as he now believed in Hob's innocence of murder, he believed in his loyalty to his friend. He wished heartily that he hadn't shown Hob so much distrust.

Hob was a sorely used boy grown to be a man. He'd had a right to hate the three men the way he had and still did. He had had a right to instill fear in them. It had been easy for him to reach a point, under Ragan's defiance and own vituperations, where he could decide to actually kill the man. But not sneakingly. It must have pained Hob to have his partner believe him capable of that. No wonder he had clammed up and refused to confide.

And now he was scheduled to be found dead under circumstances suggesting he had been responsible for the latest victims of his hero's frightened maneuvering.

Duff went back to the kitchen. Lois had freshened the fire and was drinking coffee. She got up and poured a cup for him, saying, 'Better have some. If your nerves are as bad as mine.'

'They're bad.'

He sat down across the table from her, strangely comforted to be there with her, no longer enemies. He knew she felt this, too. Color had come back into her face. Some of the old spirit was in her eyes.

She said very quietly, 'There's an ax in the woodshed. Maybe they didn't think of that.'

He dropped his hand over hers. She turned hers so that they clasped.

'Sorry, Duff. About so much.'

'Yeah.'

'I'm glad *you* don't hate me.'

'I don't think he really does.'

She shook her head wistfully. 'Fine time for me to start believing that.'

He let go of her hand and went over to the kitchen door. Through its clean glass and beyond an open space of about thirty feet, he could see the near wall of the woodshed. The door, which stood ajar, was in that wall. Peters and Higbee hadn't thought about the ax. He could see it, sunken into the chopping block.

He stood there a moment, tantalyzed yet in defeat. Peters had warned that they would be off opposite corners of the house, which would let them watch all its exits while they also kept a lookout for the new quarry they expected to arrive. There was no chance of crossing that open space and getting back with the ax. Nor would it do Hob or Ragan any good. Even if he got hold of it, he could only use it on the first gunman to come back indoors.

That would be a step toward helping Lois and, with luck, would cut the odds against them all by half. He glanced back at Lois. She was watching intently. She rose and came over behind him.

She whispered, 'Do you dare?'

'I've got to try it.'

She understood. There was no value on either of their lives, as it was. He slowly opened the door. Nothing happened, and he stepped outside.

CHAPTER EIGHTEEN

Hob didn't see the smoke piling in the distance until he came over the hump that separated Squaw Canyon from Dutch Hollow. He had done his regular riding chores that morning, his mind not on them. Then he had followed Squaw Canyon down to the deep-trenched Deschutes, not feeling like going back to camp. The contempt that had been in Duff's eyes, when he heard about the stallion, was hard to forget.

The trouble was, it kept setting up echoes in the contempt Hob felt for himself. The self-censure had begun, actually, when he realized how much he had underrated Dan Ragan. It brought back, magnified, the revulsion he had felt when he drew a bead on that stallion and pulled the trigger. It had been a fine, handsome animal. He had found it grazing peacefully. His approach hadn't alarmed it because the Ragans hadn't let it learn to distrust and fear humankind.

But he had had to do it. Much as it went against his grain, it was a shrewdly effective way to weaken Ragan and encourage him to pull out of Dutch Hollow altogether. The minute Pike mentioned it, Hob had forgotten the man Landers and the slim chance of pinning a charge of attempted murder on

Ragan. Pike had been real excited about it, but Pike wasn't the one who had to shoot the stallion in cold blood . . .

When, on the rim, Hob saw the heavy smoke, he reined in blinking his eyes. Then he went belting forward with his stomach up in his throat. He knew where the smoke came from, that he, himself, had brought it on, that Ragan had moved already to carry out his counter-threat. It was past the noon hour, and Duff should have been at the camp. They couldn't have set fire to the place with Duff still on his feet. Hob died a dozen deaths while his horse raced down the long, broken slope and hit the bottom of the hollow.

Soon he was near enough to see that nothing remained of the camp but two piles of smoldering ruins. Even the branches of some of the nearer trees were burned off.

The tired horse slowed down. Hob let it, suddenly afraid to go on in. Someone had opened the gate of the horse corral, he saw, and that puzzled him. The arsonists wouldn't have been that kind-hearted. Duff would have done it only if he knew that the barn was on fire. Maybe he hadn't been taken by complete surprise and wasn't now lying under one of those piles of smoking litter. Hob swung down from the saddle. His knees trembled. His sickened stomach threatened to bend him over at any minute.

The ruins still threw out a heat that kept

him from getting close. He moved in as near as he could, but there was no making out what all was there in the remains of the dugout. He walked over to the springs and saw fresh boot tracks that told him Duff had been there to get water. Then he saw other tracks, not as large as Duff's. Somebody had jumped him. The only question left was what had been done with him.

Hob tried to roll a cigarette but couldn't make the tobacco stay on the paper. He put the makings back in his pocket. He had found the tracks of only one man besides Duff. He didn't think that Dan Ragan had made them. For some reason, he found it hard to believe that Ragan would even have ordered a thing as malicious as this.

Lois? She had her father's stubbornness, with a temper much more explosive. She had been the one who hired Peters and Higbee to begin with. She must have liked that stallion. Women felt more affection for animals than most men did. Hob remembered how she had once threatened to give him back as good as he sent. But, no. He couldn't believe it of her, either. She just didn't know what the men she had entrusted so much to were capable of doing.

Hob didn't understand why he had this sudden faith in the Ragans. But he did know that the only real enemies he had had in Dutch Hollow were Tate Peters and Roscoe Higbee.

Born varmints, making trouble for the sake of trouble. They were the ones to find to get a line on Duff. If they had harmed Duff, he would kill them.

He picked his own and a new way to the north hollow, knowing they might be laying in wait for him along the regular trail. When he had crossed the plateau, he didn't go on to the bottom. Turning his horse west, he rode mostly under cover. But now and then he could see the horse ranch headquarters. They weren't far off from him. When he had put himself on a west quarter to the place, he stopped, dismounted and trailed reins.

Afoot, and with his gun in his hand, he moved steadily, skulking from point to point until he came to more open ground. By then he was hardly three hundred feet from the back of the house, which was as peaceful as on a Sunday morning. Shielded by the trunk of a huge, leafless tree, he studied the layout. He could see nobody. If he could make it to the back door without being discovered, he had a chance to get the jump on whoever was inside.

Even as he studied, he saw that the back door was opening, slowly and cautiously. He nearly jerked back, sure he had been spotted, when a man cut out the door and vanished into the nearby woodshed. Hob batted his eyes. Beyond a doubt, it had been Duff. He could make out Lois in the kitchen doorway. She had her hand up to her mouth. Then Duff came back in sight, running, and he carried an ax. A gun cracked, and Lois stepped forward and fairly yanked Duff inside. The door slammed shut.

Hob pulled back from sight, bewildered and given pause. They were under siege. Duff and Lois, as strange a combination as he could imagine. He understood why Duff was. But Lois? She had risked taking a shot, herself, in her frenzy to get him back indoors. Her men had turned on her. It had to be that, and because of what had happened at the cow camp and what they were doing to Duff.

Hob studied again with coldly angry eyes. One of that wolfish pair was on the far side of the woodshed, had been slow in seeing what Duff was doing. The other one had to be watching the house from this side, farther forward so that he hadn't noticed Duff or couldn't see him. Hob knew he would have been dead by now if he had made his run for that door. There was no more shooting. They seemed only to be trying to keep Duff and Lois pinned down in there. Defenseless, considering Duff's desperate move to get hold of the ax.

Hob was scratching his jaw with restless fingers when he heard the sound of hard driving hoofs to the west. He turned his head to the left, staring down the bottom. He didn't know who was coming, but he needed help. The oncomer was too far over on the bottom to be flagged down from where Hob was. Swinging, Hob made his way back to his horse as swiftly as he dared to move. Nothing happened to try to stop him. His presence there still seemed to be unknown. He mounted and cut onto the bottom. Somebody by now had heard and was watching and would see him, finally. But he had to stop whoever this was. He bore on an angle toward the other rider.

In another moment he saw that this was Dan Ragan. He didn't know what brought the man, but Ragan was trying to make it home as fast as his horse could carry him. If Peters and Higbee had turned on Lois, they had turned on Ragan automatically. Hob pulled off his hat and waved it frantically above his head. Ragan swung in the saddle to stare at him, not slowing the horse. He seemed about to pay no attention, then changed his mind and veered the horse toward Hob.

Ragan wore a gun, this time, and his hand was on its grips. His face was wary, angry. He said furiously, 'Damn you, what are you doing here?'

'Don't waste time on foolishness!' Hob returned. 'Your men have got Lois and Duff pinned down in the house!'

Ragan's eyes flashed in disdain. 'You expect me to swallow that?'

'Listen!' Hob told him about the burned cow camp and what had followed, as far as he

210

knew. 'I figured they were only holding them inside, there. But maybe they're waiting for you. Did they know you were coming out?'

Ragan still looked skeptical but less inclined to think it a trick. He shook his head. 'All I know is that Pelton sent me word Lois wanted me home on the double. I nearly killed this horse getting here.'

'Pelton? How come?'

'Said he came through here on his way home from Canyon City. Seen Lois. She asked him to send me back out quick.'

Hob had a queer feeling in his spine. Something was mighty wrong. But there was no time to pick at it. The problem at hand was almost too big, even with help from Ragan.

Ragan meant to lead, not follow. He said tersely, 'Stick that gun under your coat. Leave the holster in sight and empty. I'll ride behind you. I'll have my gun on your back.'

Hob stared in disbelief. The man was asking that he trust him with his life, in spite of the enmity between them. But it might work and save a lot of shooting that would endanger the two in the house. He opened his coat and slid the barrel of his six-shooter under the band of his pants. He swung his horse and rode ahead of Ragan.

He had a prickling between his shoulders because of Ragan, and another in his face from watching the foreground. They must have made a convincing picture. There had been no shooting when they rode into the yard between the house and barn. Then Roscoe Higbee stepped out through the barn doorway. He must have taken the shot at Duff from there. His gun rode in the holster, but he knew he would be able to fist it fast if need be. He was playing cagey until he knew what was up.

'What did you catch yourself, Dan?' he called. There was a grin of satisfaction on his face.

'Where's Peters?' Ragan returned.

'Far side of the house. Doncaster's holed up in there. He's holding Miss Lois hostage. We ain't been able to do a thing.'

From where he had been hiding, Hob realized, Higbee hadn't seen them down the bottom. Ragan pretended to believe him and snapped, 'Swing down, Loman.'

Hob obeyed, trying to guess what Ragan wanted from him next. As he came down on the blind side of his horse, he knew. His hand snaked under his coat for his gun. He stepped around the horse with the gun lined on Higbee.

'Quiet, man,' he advised. 'One peep out of you, and you're dead.'

Higbee didn't yell a warning to Peters, but he ducked back into the barn. His gun exploded, and Hob felt the whisper of death in his ear. But it was better to have the killer in there than between Hob and the house.

He yelled, 'Look out for Peters!' at Ragan,

then threw himself sidewise and sprinted to the wall of the barn. The wall was tight boards-and-bats, but he kept moving, giving Higbee no chance to spot and drill him through the wall.

There was a window ahead of him, a port used for cleaning stalls. He reached it, stopped and listened, hearing nothing inside or out. He risked a look through the window. Higbee was crouched over there beside the door. An upright timber stood in the way of a shot at him. Hardly breathing, Hob pulled himself up into the window, swung his legs inside, and let himself down to the floor.

For a moment he was half-blinded, for Ragan hadn't put many windows in his barn. Hob waited a moment, his breathing shallow and quiet. There had been no more shooting after Higbee's one vicious shot. He wondered what Ragan was doing. Higbee wondered, too. He was crouched there, unsuspecting of what was behind him, yet unable to take a look out the door.

Hob slipped stealthily toward him, his eyes focused better. He was remembering how this man had held Duff's arms while Peters beat his face, belly and ribs to a pulp. He was remembering his own responsibility for the whole thing.

He spoke quietly. 'Higbee, drop that gun.'

Higbee hauled around, his gun spitting flame. Above it, Hob saw the wild, unrelenting face of a killer. He felt a bullet bite into him just as he shot back. Then they stood there, jarring the barn with thunder, hurling bolts of lightning at one another. He still felt no pain when he saw Higbee fold slowly over and go down. Then there was more shooting, somewhere outside, several quick shots. He lurched over to Higbee. The man made an effort to lift up his gun.

He said, 'Goddamn you, Loman,' and went limp.

Hob took the gun from a loosened hand and tossed it off into the obscurity. He staggered to the door and looked out, a hand clasping his shoulder, where his shirt had grown wet. The other shooting had stopped, he realized. There was nothing to see on this side of the house. Even the horses they had ridden in had bolted away. He stood inside the barn to pluck live cartridges from his belt and replace the empties in the gun. The wet arm felt funny but he could use it and the hand.

He began to make sense of the other shooting. Ragan had gone around the house and flushed Peters. Hob wished he knew how it had turned out, who would be waiting when he went around there, himself. He staggered out into the open. All at once he tensed and nearly shot. But the figure hurrying around the corner of the house toward him was Ragan. Walking more openly but still looking grim.

Ragan said in his heavy voice, 'Couldn't

214

stop him. He made a dive for the back door and got into the house. Get under cover. He'll be shooting at us in a minute.'

It filtered into Hob's dazed mind that Ragan was talking about Peters. Ragan half dragged him back into the barn. The grimness of the situation began to reach Hob. Peters would use Lois and Duff to protect himself. Shooting at the house from outside was out of the question.

Ragan looked down at the body on the barn floor. He looked up at Hob. 'You hit bad?'

'Just a scratch.'

'You're bleeding like a stuck hog.'

Hob remembered something and said, 'Duff got himself an ax. I seen him. Just before you come along.'

'I hope to hell he's handy with it.'

'Yeah.'

CHAPTER NINETEEN

It was queer, when it might be ticking off the last of their lives, that time could drag so heavily. Duff knew it must be wearing equally on the men waiting outside for their next victims to show up. Lois, too, showed the strain, although for a while she had thrown it off. And then, because of the silence and their intent listening, they heard horses coming on from down the hollow.

Duff slipped to a window and pushed the curtain aside an inch or two. He didn't realize that Lois was right behind him until he heard her gasp.

'No, dad! No!'

Hob rode between them and the barn. Ragan came behind him, with a gun trained on Hob's back. The stubborn man was delivering not only himself but Hob into their hands.

Lois moaned, 'Oh, the fool!'

And then they saw Higbee appear in the barn doorway and call to Ragan. The two exchanged remarks, and Ragan seemed to have no idea of his fatal blunder. Then Ragan said something to Hob, and Hob swung down on the near side of his horse. And then Duff knew that he and Lois had done her father a gross injustice. Hob had fisted a gun. Duff

216

swung her back from the window just as a shot rang out there.

'Down flat!'

She obeyed, but there was a shine in her eyes and new color surged into her cheeks. Neither of them understood it, but Hob and Ragan had worked together, and they had been smarter than the killers. There had been only the one shot, and Duff turned back to the window in time to see Hob sliding along the wall of the barn. Ragan had swung off his horse and disappeared. The horses had scampered away. Higbee seemed to have ducked back into the barn. Hob was after him, and Duff wondered about Peters.

He had to rush into a bedroom for a look at the other side of the house. It was Lois's room, frilly and pretty, with a woman look and feel. He made a crack in the curtains there and in a moment had spotted Ragan. The man had slipped in behind a tree on that side and was probing the area roundabout with his eyes. Duff couldn't spot Peters, either. There were too many places where he could be hiding.

He yearned for a firearm to help Ragan, but all he had was the ax lying on the kitchen table. A useless thing now, although a while before it had seemed precious. Ragan kept trying to locate his man, but Peters kept lying doggo. And then a brisk firing broke out toward the barn. It seemed to flush Peters, at last, for Ragan stepped out quickly and shot. Peters fired back, and then Ragan was shooting steadily, looking toward the back corner of the house.

Duff wheeled and raced to the kitchen and grabbed the ax. He was standing to one side of the door, flattened to the wall, when Peters reached it. Duff watched the knob turn. Then the door swung open, and Peters stepped in, sweeping the rifle barrel back and forth. All he saw was Lois on the floor. She lifted her head and stared up at him, trying to hold his attention as long as she could.

Duff brought down the ax, but he didn't drive it into the man's head. He wanted at least one of them alive, for only they could convince Hob of the truth about Pelton. The metal head of the ax crashed against the stock of the rifle, which flew from Peter's hands. Peters cursed and made a dive for it, but Duff straightened him with a jerk and whipped him around. A fist arced quick and hard, clipping the man's jaw. Peters grunted and staggered back, blinking his eyes, bewildered by surprise. He cast a look at the rifle, but Lois scrambled forward and jerked it away.

Peters made an animal sound and lashed out with his fists. Then he tried to grab up the ax that Duff had dropped. Duff hauled him upright and nearly broke his hand on the man's mouth. Lois could have taken over then. She had sprung to her feet, but the rifle was pointed at the floor. Peters straightened himself once more. He drove forward, but Duff met him with a hard punch to the belly. Peters gagged and clutched himself with both hands. He was a gunman and bully. Without a gun or somebody's help, he was nothing at all. He wheeled and dove for the door.

Lois fired, but into the floor. Peters didn't see that. He turned toward her, lifting his hands over his head.

He said abjectly, 'All right.'

He still had a feeble hope of help from Higbee, if Higbee was still able to help. There had been no shooting outside since the flurry when Peters made his run for the house. Duff made him sit down in the kitchen chair. He used the man's belt and his own to lash Peters' hands together behind the chair back. He picked up the ax and gave it to Lois, taking the rifle from her.

'If he makes a move, brain him,' he said.

She nodded. Her expression convinced even Peters that she would do it.

Duff slipped out the back way, holding the rifle at ready. The question now was Higbee. He stepped around the corner of the house and looked toward the barn. In a moment his heart leaped. Hob and Ragan had seen him and were coming out of the barn doorway. He knew they had been rendered helpless with Peters inside the house. They still didn't know what the one rifle shot, in there, had meant. Duff waited while they came hurrying toward him. He saw the stain on Hob's shirt. But they walked openly, which meant that Higbee didn't have to be considered, anymore. Hob grinned at Duff as they came up, but he looked woozy. Ragan rushed on into the house with Hob right behind him.

Duff didn't know which face drew him the strongest when Hob and Lois looked at each other. Her eyes shot to the blood on Hob's shirt, and she paled. She looked back at Hob's face. He had brought a cautious sternness to it. She noticed this, grew somber, and gave a slight toss of the head. They were out of immediate danger, and much lay between them unresolved.

Then Hob said, 'Howdy, Lois.'

She said, 'Hello, Hob.'

And slowly they smiled.

'He's hurt, girl,' Ragan said briskly. 'We need clean cloth and hot water.'

He seemed not to like what he had seen between the two, just then.

Higbee's slug had drilled through the fleshy, underarm side of Hob's shoulder. It had narrowly missed the joint and an impact that could have crippled him for life. Ragan cleaned, disinfected and dressed the wound. He was good at it, although his practice had been on horses. Peters sat slumped and solemn throughout, his last hope vanished.

And then Duff knew they had come to the most difficult part of it. Even Ragan didn't know the extent to which Pike Pelton had figured in the trouble.

Walking over to Peters, Duff said roughly, 'There are two men here who would string you up in a minute if they knew what you intended to do to this girl. Supposing you make it easier on yourself. Tell them who you were really working for.'

Peters wet his lips with his tongue. Duff's hint at threatened molestation had brought a look of fury to Hob's face, even to Ragan's.

Peters said thickly, 'Pelton.'

'Doing what?' Duff pressed.

'You know as well as I do what.'

'But these men don't know. Tell 'em.'

Peters sighed. 'We was to get them two in a gun ruckus, one way or another. Pike figured it was sure shot that Loman would kill the old duffer.'

'And why did Pelton want Ragan dead?'

'He knew too much. Then it was pretty sure that the girl did. And you, too. He decided it was time to get the lot of you off his mind.'

Duff looked at Hob 'You want to ask him any questions?' Hob looked sick. He shook his head.

'You, Ragan?' Duff asked.

Ragan said in an all gone voice, 'Who killed Frank Fleeson and Vince Mounts?'

'Pelton.'

Ragan looked as stunned as Hob did. Ragan had the most to take into account. Truths he had not let himself entertain because they would destroy his own truths. His easy, cut and dried beliefs still struggled to survive.

As though still trying to sidestep the issue, he said, 'I'll go back to town and bring out the sheriff.'

'I'll go,' Duff said.

Ragan shook his head. 'You fellas stay here with Lois. We might not have seen the last of this.'

'That made sense. It would be highly dangerous for Ragan, with night not far away, to try to take Peters in to the sheriff without help. Hob looked too shaky to go along with him, or to be left behind to guard Peters and protect Lois if Duff went with Ragan.

'How about Pelton?' Duff asked. 'You going to bring charges against him?'

'That's up to Brig Langford,' Ragan said coldly. 'He can question this man and decide how much he wants to believe.'

'*You* don't believe it?' Lois gasped.

'I never said that.'

Ragan left.

Duff told Hob about the letter, then, and how strongly it suggested what really happened to Amos Bickle. Hob's face hardly changed at all. It was his hands, while he sat there in the chair where Ragan had dressed his wound, that told Duff how deeply it had gone in. They were fisted, and the knuckles were white.

He looked at Lois and said in a stranger's voice, 'And you knew about that all along.'

Lois started to speak, but Duff cut in. 'She hadn't the slightest idea of it till I told her, here in this room today. Mandy told me only a few nights back. She didn't know about it till Fleeson told her, right after Mounts was killed.'

Hob sat unmoving in the chair. The hatred he seemed to have rid himself of for a while was back multiplied. Ragan's contribution to that old miscarriage of justice seemed all the worse now. And now the hate must include Pike Pelton, false friend and idol of clay feet.

Lois said quietly, 'I'm not going to let you hate *me* again, Hob. When I saw my father close his mind to the possibility that he might have made a mistake, it opened my eyes. He appointed that court, all men of his own bent. Your father was up against a bigotry and prejudice that gave him no chance. They were weaker men than Burley Loman, all of them. Afraid of him. Maybe that's why their judgment was so harsh. I don't think I'm like that, but I believed in my father. I didn't know yet that admitting a mistake is a bigger thing than never making one. I made the worst one of my life when I laughed at your rage, back there. I don't expect you ever to like me again. But I do ask something. Forgive me?'

Hob looked up at her in amazement. Lois crawling at last, the thing he had wanted to see? He knew it wasn't crawling. Lois had only spoken from her heart. He didn't say anything, but something had softened slightly in his eyes.

Lois turned, went to the stove and poked in more firewood. The day was all but gone. Ragan wouldn't reach town until after dark, and Duff doubted that the sheriff would be out before morning. That meant standing guard—over Peters all night, and Duff knew that the man was watching every moment that passed for a chance to make a break. Not only was he a man who needed to be removed from circulation for the sake of society. Without him, the case against Pike Pelton would be weakened badly.

'Any place we can lock this fella up, Lois?' Duff asked.

'Not that I'd rely on to hold him.'

She was starting supper. Hob watched her, as though struck by the oddity of it, as Duff was himself. Only that morning nothing could have seemed a more remote possibility than that she would be doing this. That he and Hob would be here with her, united in a common effort if in no other way. Then Hob got to his feet.

'We're going to have to nighthcrd the buzzard,' he said, with a nod at Peters. 'And I still feel a little woozy. Reckon I'll go over to the haymow and catch some sleep so I can spell you later.'

'Good idea,' Duff agreed.

'You don't have to go over there,' Lois objected. 'There are beds in the house.'

'Reckon I'd feel more at home in the barn.'

Lois frowned. 'Don't you want something to eat?'

'Not hungry.'

She bit her lip. He was refusing her hospitality. Duff hoped he liked the company of the dead man in the barn. He went out, and Duff sat down across the table from Peters.

'I gotta set like this all night?' Peters complained. 'My arms are killing me, already.'

'That's too damned bad.'

Lois turned from the stove. 'Couldn't we loosen them for a while, Duff? We've got to give him something to eat, anyhow.'

'You can't be kind to this kind of animal,' Duff told her. 'He's trying for a break, and he can set there till his arms fall off.'

Peters muttered a curse that confirmed Duff's opinion. Duff wished they had sent Lois to town with her father. If Peters could get his hands on her and use her as a hostage, he would have things his own way. And Pelton was still free to move about. If he chanced to see Ragan, he would know that the trap hadn't worked. If he came back to check

'Duff!' Lois exclaimed. She was staring out the window. 'Hob's got a horse!'

Duff swung over to where she stood and looked out. There had been several saddled horses scattered around. He had intended to take care of them, cover Higbee's body, and do any other necessary chores when Hob got back to guard Peters. Just as he looked out the window, Hob rode by, moving quietly, hoping to get away unseen. Duff lunged to the door and shouted. Hob only drove in his spurs.

'He's going after Pelton,' Lois moaned. 'And my father, too. Oh, Duff. Stop him.'

'I can't leave you here with Peters.'

'You've got to.'

Duff knew it was true. It would be the ultimate tragedy if Hob turned killer at this point. He had to be stopped. But he couldn't leave Peters with Lois, and taking him along would slow him so he could never overtake Hob.

'Fetch me rope,' he snapped.

Lois understood and dashed out through the back door. Duff loosened the belts that had bound Peters' wrists to the rungs of the chair back. He stepped away quickly and picked up the rifle that was the only weapon there. The man was too stiff to try anything at the moment. He winced when he got to his feet. Lois was back in a moment with a couple of catch ropes. Duff ordered Peters into Ragan's bedroom.

'Stretch out on that bed.'

'Hey, now—'

'Flatten yourself, damn you. I don't much care if I have to kill you, instead.'

Peters groaned and obeyed. Lois helped

Duff spread-eagle and lash him down there. They made the knots strong and used plenty of rope.

'I can handle him now,' Lois said. 'You get going.'

'I'm not leaving you anywhere close to this fella. You're coming with me.'

It would be a long ride, most of it after dark, and it would be cold. He told her to put on a warm coat and wrap something warm around her head. Because of the delay imposed by Peters, there was small chance of catching Hob before he reached town. The only hope was of stopping him, there, before he had done anything.

It took more time to get horses. Duff would have preferred his own, but it was nowhere in sight. The horses Peters and Higbee had used that day, still saddled, were used to the barn and had come in. He took one of them. Lois wanted her own horse, which was in the corral. He helped her saddle it. He took a moment more to go in the barn and throw a saddle blanket over Higbee's body.

And then he and Lois were riding swiftly into the looming twilight.

CHAPTER TWENTY

Night was full when they came onto the portage road from the Deschutes landing to Dalles City. Ahead lay the long, twisting miles of the canyons. That would make for even slower going, for there would be frozen stretches down there pretty soon. Duff rode with mounting discouragement. The horse that Lois rode was small but it had plenty of bottom, and she kept up with him without effort. The loneliness of the uplands was as oppressive as the growing chill of the night. Only now and then did they see the light of some human habitation, off at distances.

The dark canyons were as bad as he had expected. Freezing had set in, and stretches that had been damp were slick and treacherous. Hob hadn't had to put up with ice, and this was throwing them farther and farther behind him.

And then Lois broke a long and total silence, calling, 'Duff, I'm sure my father would have returned tonight, even if Brig Langford waits till morning. We should have met him by now, and we haven't.'

He had hoped she wouldn't think of that. It seemed probable to him, too, that Ragan would have come back to the ranch the soonest possible. It would take a lot of faith to

228

leave Lois alone out there with two men he had feared so long, and Peters, besides, any longer than he had to. Duff shared her fear that Hob had something to do with preventing his return. There was no sense in reassuring her when there was no telling what they would find in town, so he didn't answer her.

It seemed to take forever to reach the Columbia. But from there on the going was much better. Duff knew that Lois shared his mounting dread. They wound along under the great headland, and at last came around the point into town. The scene along the street was tranquil enough to make their concern seem foolish.

They had gone a couple of blocks, slowed to a walk, when Duff pulled in. Lois stopped and looked at him inquiringly. 'You go to your town house,' he said, 'and see if your dad's there. I'm going to the wagon yard.'

He knew she would rather stay with him, but she nodded her head. 'If you think that's best.'

'If he's not there, you stay anyhow. I'll be over as soon as I can make it.'

She shook her head. 'I couldn't bear to be alone. I'll go to Mandy's house.'

'Mandy?' He stared. 'I thought she'd gone.'

'Not yet.'

Duff asked her how to find her house, which he had never visited. Then he rode on. He came to the other edge of town, and a moment later reined in outside the high wall of the wagon yard. Its gate was shut. He swung down and walked to it to find that it was barred on the inside.

Not knowing if this should assure or alarm him, Duff put his eye to a crack in the fence. There was no light in Pelton's quarters and office structure, just beyond the fence. But the gate was barred from inside. He went on along the fence, wondering if there was a way to get in and out that he hadn't noticed on his few short visits. Around the corner in the fence he found it, an entrance hardly larger than the door of a house. It unlatched and opened readily, and he stepped through.

The whole yard was dark, and the ride down the lighted street had thrown his eyes a little off focus. The barn was to his right, and along that fence were several spare wagons. On the other side, by the big gate, was the office and quarters shack. There was clutter along that fence, too, and across the far end of the yard. His vision improved, and he started forward, only to haul up, arrested in his tracks.

The corner of the barn had cut it off until he had moved forward a dozen steps. There in the dark angle formed by barn and fence stood a wagon with a reared-up tongue. And something dangled from the upper end of the tongue.

Duff couldn't bring himself to go over there. He knew he had to, and after a moment made his legs move again. It had taken a big and powerful man to upend that tongue, burdened the way it was. Or maybe it had been upended first, with the rope laced through the iron loop on its end. And then a jerk and a heave that had lifted Pike Pelton as near to heaven as he would ever come. Up there into a frightening duplication of the way Burley Loman met death.

He stood for long moments, there at the end of everything for Hob and himself, as well as for Pelton. Then he turned and left the yard, closing the gate behind him. He wasn't going to report his find. Teamsters and barnhands would show up there by sunup. He walked back to his horse and swung into the saddle. Hob had done this and then headed for yonder. He had the rest of the night to get a start. Sickened though he was, Duff wished him luck.

He rode to the Ragan house, following the directions Lois had given him. The whole house was dark. Even so, he went onto the porch and rapped loudly on the door. There was no response. He went on to Mandy's, leaving the horse at the rear end of the footbridge and going on afoot.

Lois was waiting for him. She opened the door the minute she heard his bootfalls on the porch. She took one look at his face and pressed a hand to her mouth. She stepped back silently for him to enter. Mandy stood there in the room. She looked worried and yet seemed glad to see him again. He was glad she hadn't left the country yet, although it could only afford him one more look at her.

'Pelton's dead,' he said. 'Strung up on a wagon tongue.'

'Then,' Lois faltered, 'where's Dad?'

The question checked Duff's breath. In his own shock he hadn't thought of Ragan, himself. He hadn't gone back to Dutch Hollow. He hadn't been at his house. Duff knew he couldn't give Hob the head start he had intended. Hob might not have left town yet, might be hunting Ragan at that moment. Meaning to square the whole account in one violent night. As long as there was a chance he hadn't yet found Ragan, it had to be reported to the law and the hunt started for Hob.

Duff didn't want to do it. He knew he had no choice.

Lois sank into a chair, at the end of her own rope. Duff turned and walked out, and Mandy followed him to the porch.

'I couldn't go,' she said quietly. 'And I'll be here. Remember that.'

He rode to the courthouse to see Hob's horse racked on the street in front.

For a moment Duff couldn't believe it. But there was no mistake. Hob had turned himself in. Stunned now beyond thought, Duff swung his own mount and rode back over to Main. That settled it. Hob had done what he had lived for. That had ended his interest in life. For one of the few times in his own life, Duff really wanted a drink. He stopped in front of the Mount Hood, tied his horse and went in. He wondered if Hob had the killing of Ragan to answer for, also. He had his drink and then a second, feeling neither.

He went back to the street and there, coming along, was Hob. Duff let out a yell that drew his attention. When he rode over to the edge of the sidewalk, Hob's face was dark with anger.

'Did you leave Lois alone out there?' he demanded.

Duff could hardly find his voice. 'She's at Mandy's.' And then the unbearable question, 'Where's Dan Ragan?'

'When I left Langford's office, they were taking him on to the jail.'

'Ragan?' Duff saw it, then, the terrible cycle of Ragan's stern justice come full circle. '*He* hung Pelton.'

'So you were at the wagonyard, too.'

'I was.'

Hob swung down, tied his horse and stepped onto the walk. They went over and sat down on the bench in front of the saloon. Hob rolled a cigarette. His fingers trembled. He wasn't as unshaken by it as he tried to pretend.

'I was going to kill Pelton. Not that way, but kill him. Then I found him. I knew who'd beat me there. I went over to Ragan's house. He was there in a daze. He'd done it and didn't know what to do next. I offered to help him get out of the country. But that dogged set to him was too much. He said justice had to be done. I thought he was talking about Pelton. He was. And he wasn't.'

56267